Disney

HIGH SCHOOL MUSICAL

STORIES FROM EAST HIGH SUPER SPECIAL

SHINING MOMENTS

HIGH SCHOOL MUSICAL

STORIES FROM EAST HIGH SUPER SPECIAL

SHINING MOMENTS

By Helen Perelman

Based on the Disney Channel Original Movie
"High School Musical," Written by Peter Barsocchini
Based on "High School Musical 2," Written by Peter Barsocchini
Based on "High School Musical 3: Senior Year," Written by Peter Barsocchini
Based on Characters Created by Peter Barsocchini

New York

HIGH SCHOOL MUSICAL

STORIES FROM EAST HIGH SUPER SPECIAL

SHINING MOMENTS

CHAPTER ONE

Gabriella Montez smiled as her best friend, Taylor McKessie, stood up to address a group of East High seniors. They were sitting in the cafeteria after school for their first senior-project committee meeting. Everyone was excited about planning the upcoming senior class spring event.

"Our senior project has to be something *spectacular*," Taylor, clutching her clipboard tightly, told the group. "This is one of the last senior activities of the year, and we *have* to get this project right. We need to do something that says we care and that we're dedicated to our community."

"Really?" Jason Cross complained. He stuffed his hands into his varsity basketball sweatshirt pockets and leaned back in his chair. "There's so much that we all have to do before graduation. And we've all submitted our college applications already. We won't even be able to get any acknowledgment for it."

"Not everything we do is for the record," Taylor said crisply.

Gabriella looked over at Taylor and smiled. She took a different approach with Jason.

"Our senior project is a chance for us to make a difference," Gabriella told him. "We should give back to our community." She looked around at her friends. "Plus, it will be fun!"

Taylor nodded. "And so," she went on, "we need—"

"East High seniors rock!" Chad Danforth

yelled as he bounded into the room with his best friend, Troy Bolton, close behind him. Chad dribbled his basketball and faked shooting a basket. "Let's slam-dunk this senior project!"

"Go, Wildcats!" Troy cheered. Then he sat down next to Gabriella. He winked at her and gave her shoulder a playful tap.

Taylor glared at Chad and Troy for interrupting her opening remarks, but then a smile quickly spread across her face.

"Yes, let's make sure that this year's project is our winning shot, a slam dunk!" she exclaimed, grinning.

Gabriella laughed. Last year, Taylor never would have even known what a slam dunk was—or even that a basketball game was scored by earning two points for each basket. Senior year was different for everyone at East High.

For Gabriella, there was so much about East High that was still new. She had arrived at the school in the second semester of junior year, after a fun ski vacation with her mom. It wasn't skiing that made the trip so fantastic—it was meeting Troy Bolton! When they ended up on stage together singing karaoke at the resort's New Year's Eve party, everything changed. Singing together had been incredible—and they both knew they'd never be the same. Neither of them had any idea that Gabriella would be attending East High. And Gabriella was shocked to learn that Troy was not the head of the Drama Club but the captain of the basketball team! And Troy couldn't believe how one girl could open his eyes to a part of school that he had hardly thought about—the stage! After lots of starts and stops, they had finally ended up onstage together again in the East High musical *Twinkle Towne*! And the rest was history!

Troy always said that it was Gabriella who brought the school together and united everyone— whether they played on the basketball team or were members of the Scholastic Decathlon team. Because of her, people at East High started realizing that they were more alike than they had ever imagined. People also began to confess their other interests, such as baking and dancing. The fact that Taylor McKessie, the president of the Chemistry Club and the Scholastic Decathlon team, would become friends with Chad, the co-captain of the varsity basketball team, was a pretty good example of how Gabriella had encouraged everyone to be more open and accepting of each other. But Troy knew that for Gabriella, it was all about being with her friends and seeing people happy.

Taylor continued with her speech to the committee. "And so, now it's our time to give back," she said, smiling at her friends sitting around the cafeteria.

"Let's do this!" Martha Cox cheered from her seat.

The twenty or so students on the committee all eagerly nodded their heads in agreement. Taylor's enthusiasm was contagious! Everyone there wanted to make sure this year's senior project was ultra special.

"Last year's senior class," Taylor said, "did

an unbelievable job of cleaning up a park downtown. And two years ago, the seniors helped build houses for hurricane victims."

"That's amazing," Kelsi Nielsen commented. "We should definitely do something like that for the community."

Taylor smiled. That was exactly the kind of response that she was looking for! When Ms. Darbus had asked her to chair this committee, she felt honored. She was already involved with many senior-year activities, but the senior project was a huge deal. The project represented the graduating class, and was, hopefully, a lasting gift to the community. Taylor wanted to make sure that this year's senior class would be a part of one of the best projects in the history of East High!

"Now the hard part is narrowing down the ideas and then presenting them to the class," Taylor explained. "We should come up with a list and then present it on Friday. There will be a vote in homeroom, and the decision will be announced later that day."

"Sounds like a great plan, Taylor," Troy said. He flashed her a smile. "You have my vote!"

"Thanks, Troy," Taylor said. "But try thinking of stuff we can do. Your pal Chad has already mentioned cleaning up the town junkyard!" She walked over and gave Chad a gentle tap on the head.

Chad grinned. "I thought everyone would love cleaning up the junkyard. It would be a totally rockin' party!"

"That's not exactly helping out the community, Chad," Gabriella said with a smile. "I know how much the place means to you and Troy, but I'm pretty sure it's going to stay a junkyard for years to come."

"It'd better!" Troy exclaimed, leaping up to hit a high five with Chad. "That place holds a ton of history that should never go away!"

Taylor shook her head. "All right," she told the group, trying to get everyone to focus on the issue at hand. "Thank you so much for coming today. Please think about locations around town

7

where you think we can make a difference, and let me know."

"Thanks, Taylor!" Martha called out as she walked out of the cafeteria. "I'll give you a list of ideas in the morning!"

"I can give you a list, too," Chad said. "But first, I need an afternoon snack to give me some energy to think!"

Taylor gave Chad a playful shove as she grabbed her bag. "It's going to take lots of snacking, huh?" she joked.

"This is going to be fantastic," Gabriella told Troy as she gathered up her books.

"You say that about every senior activity," Troy said, laughing. "You and Taylor are definitely the head of the senior *cheer* committee."

Gabriella shrugged. "Well, it's nice to feel some school spirit," she admitted. "I've never felt this attached to a school before, and I want to do something good for the community." She had moved around a lot as a kid and was never in any place long enough to have real ties. This past year had been a real change of pace. East High really felt like home to her.

"Is it just the school that you're attached to?" Troy said with a playful nudge.

"Oh, you are a crazy Wildcat!" Gabriella exclaimed, giggling. She knew that Troy understood and felt the same way she did. "Come on, let's catch up with Chad and Taylor and grab something to eat," she said as she grabbed Troy's hand and then ran to meet up with their friends.

After the four friends had grabbed a slice of pizza, Troy drove Gabriella to the Wellington Community Center. Gabriella loved to swim, and the center had a great indoor pool perfect for doing laps.

Troy pulled up to the front door in his beat-up truck. "I used to come here as a kid," he said. "Back then it wasn't a community center. It was a theater. My parents used to take me every year during the holidays to see *A Christmas Carol*."

"I didn't even know that there was a theater

here," Gabriella said. She usually just went straight to the locker room and pool and didn't take the time to explore the old building behind the recreation center.

Troy shrugged. "There hasn't been a show here for years. I think they lost funding or something," he told her. "Then the city bought the building and turned the place into a community center for families in the neighborhood."

"Interesting," Gabriella said slowly. She looked over at Troy, her brown eyes sparkling. "Are you thinking what I'm thinking?"

Troy looked at Gabriella's face as a smile started to form there. "Senior project?" Troy asked, raising one eyebrow. "I wonder what we could do. But I have a feeling that when I talk to you later tonight you're going to have it all figured out."

Gabriella grinned and jumped out of the truck. "I'll call you later, Wildcat. Thanks for the ride." She walked into the center, thinking about what Troy had told her. A theater? she wondered. She was surprised she had never seen that part of the building. Before she went into the locker room, the gymnasium doors caught her eye. They were usually closed, but today they were wide open. Gabriella couldn't help but peek inside.

"I wish we could play against them," she over-heard a little girl with a long brown ponytail say.

"But we're terrible!" a boy responded. He had a sad look on his face. "We need some help. A coach would be nice, you know?"

"If we're going to play, we need help!" the little girl exclaimed, breaking away to shoot the ball she was holding. It went flying and swished through the net above her head.

Hmm, thought Gabriella. Did I just stumble on a potential senior project? I might just have the help you are looking for, she mused, as she watched the kids play. Some basketball players, some theater people, and some enthusiastic seniors looking for their class project? She grinned as she thought of all the help the senior

11

class of East High could bring to the center. Now she just had to convince Taylor and the rest of the senior class that the center could really use their help—*and* that helping out there would be a great idea for a senior project!

CHAPTER TWO

On Monday morning, Gabriella and Taylor sat in the cafeteria, anxiously waiting for Principal Matsui to arrive. All the seniors had gathered in the cafeteria before homeroom to hear about two senior projects. Taylor had narrowed down everyone's ideas and selected two to present to the senior class. The voting would take place during homeroom. While Taylor loved the Wellington Community Center idea, Hilary Lloyd, one of the seniors on the committee, wanted to clean up a downtown park by planting flowers and fixing up the playground, and Taylor thought that was a possible idea. Hilary had the flu, so Taylor would be presenting her idea for her. The idea of cleaning up that park was good, but Taylor thought it was too similar to last year's senior class project. She wanted this year to be different. Plus, the community center had opportunities for lots of Wildcats to get involved.

Taylor smiled over at Gabriella. "Don't worry," Taylor whispered. "Your idea is totally a slam dunk!" She winked at her friend. Gabriella looked over at Taylor and took a deep breath. She really hoped the seniors would choose her idea.

After Gabriella had finished swimming that day, she had explored the old building. She noticed that the game room was in desperate need of a paint job. And the theater looked like no one had been on the stage in years! Gabriella had talked to Mr. Davis, the director of the center, and he thought her idea was a great one. Now all she had to do was convince the senior class. She was really nervous!

Looking around the cafeteria at all the seniors, she hoped that she could convey to her classmates how much the center needed them. Those kids at the center were in need of some Wildcat spirit! Gabriella knew that all her friends would be able to help. She tried to be confident and hoped everyone would agree that the Wellington Community Center would be the perfect choice for this year's senior project.

"Good morning, students!" Principal Matsui announced, walking into the cafeteria. "Let's get started, shall we?" He looked over at the committee members and smiled. "We have two people from the senior project committee here this morning to read you the descriptions of the two projects to vote on. Please fill out your ballots and give them to your homeroom teachers. We'll announce the project during fifth period." He looked up and grinned at Taylor and Gabriella. "Please give Taylor McKessie and Gabriella Montez your undivided attention."

Taylor flipped through her binder and found Hilary's notes about her project idea. She walked up to the front of the room. "Good morning, East High seniors!" Taylor began. "The park downtown needs our help," she read.

Gabriella tried to concentrate on Taylor's speech, but she was distracted by something she saw out of the corner of her eye. Troy was smiling at her from across the room, giving her a thumbs-up. She gave him a grateful smile. His support made her feel stronger and more confident.

After Taylor had finished speaking, Gabriella stood up and approached the podium. "The kids at the Wellington Community Center need us," Gabriella said into the microphone. She took a deep breath and continued on. "With our skills as basketball players, musical theater performers, artists, and helpful students, we can make a difference to this center. I hope that you'll vote to be a part of this senior project."

Sharpay Evans, who had been doodling in her

notebook with a bright pink pen, suddenly looked up. "Did I hear you say 'musical *theater* performers'? Now *that* is a great idea for a volunteer project," she commented loudly. She tossed her blond hair back and smiled.

Sharpay's twin brother, Ryan Evans, was excited to hear that bit of news, too. "What an awesome idea," he said.

Gabriella looked over at Ryan and smiled. She was thrilled that other people were seeing the great possibilities of the project.

Principal Matsui looked over at the seniors and smiled. "Okay, students. Please report to homeroom, and don't forget to vote!" Taylor turned to Gabriella and held up both her hands to show that her fingers were crossed.

Later that day, during fifth period, when most of the senior class was back in the cafeteria for lunch, the speakers throughout the school cracked and buzzed. Taylor grabbed Gabriella's hand. "Here comes the announcement!" she cried out.

Gabriella anxiously looked up toward the speaker at the top of the steps in the cafeteria. She hoped that the rest of the senior class was going to agree with her about the choice for their class project.

"We are pleased to report that this year's senior project will be volunteering at the Wellington Community Center!" Principal Matsui announced. "Please sign up for the project with Taylor McKessie. Good luck—and have fun!"

"All right!" Troy cheered. He grinned at Gabriella across the cafeteria table. "This is going to be a cool project. Not only for us, but for all those kids."

Taylor took out a stack of papers from her clipboard. "Here are the sign-up sheets," she said. She pushed her lunch tray out of the way, making room on the table. She shrugged as Troy raised one eyebrow suspiciously. "What? I like to be prepared. And we really don't have much time. Last night Gabriella and I came up with a few different committees for the project, just in case it got picked."

"You wasted no time, huh?" Chad asked, amazed at Taylor's organizational skills. He took a bite of his turkey sandwich and shook his head. It never ceased to amaze him how prepared Taylor was for everything!

Taylor gave Chad a small smile and pulled out the different sheets. "We have tutoring, painting the game room, being part of a musical show, teaching swimming, and of course, coaching basketball."

"Sign me up for hoops!" Chad exclaimed. "I have some choice moves for those kids."

"You know it!" Jason exclaimed, coming over just in time to sign his name. "I'm going to channel Coach Bolton." He straightened up and lowered his voice. "Drills give us the skills to work as a team," he said, echoing a line that all the players had heard their coach say many times.

Troy and Chad laughed. Jason passed the sheet to Chad, who also gladly signed his name.

"What about you, Zeke?" Jason asked. He

leaned over to the table next to them. "Can we count on you?"

"Sure, I'll help out on the court," Zeke Baylor said. He had another idea, too. He grinned at his friends as he confessed his thoughts. "I would love to see what the kitchen is like there. Maybe I could help develop some snack ideas for the kids. You know, nutritious can be delicious!"

Gabriella laughed. "If anyone can figure out how to make something delicious, it would be you," she said. Zeke was not only a great basketball player, but he was an amazing baker.

"Sign me up to help paint the game room," Martha said, rushing over to Taylor. "The kids and I can come up with an idea to paint something really cool, like a mural!"

Gabriella turned to Martha. "That's a great idea! Thanks so much," she said, giving her a wide smile.

Just then, Sharpay came rushing over, the heels of her pink feathered mules tapping against the floor. "*Obviously* I will be helping out with the musical," she said grandly. "What would a musical be without me? Every show needs a star," she added with a wink.

"Sign me up for that, too, Taylor," Ryan said, as he walked over to the table. "Maybe the kids would be interested in learning some cool tap-dance moves."

Taylor nodded and jotted down some notes. Then she took a stack of the committee sheets and started to walk around to all the tables in the cafeteria to hand out the sign-up sheets.

As Taylor walked away, Troy leaned in closer to Gabriella. "What are you going to do for the project? Have you decided whether to sign up for tutoring or to coach swimming?"

"I'm going to see about volunteering for the swim program," Gabriella told him. She had been thinking how she really missed teaching swimming to little kids. Last summer, when she was the lifeguard at the Lava Springs Country Club, she had loved working with the young kids who came to the pool. She glanced over at Troy.

"I don't think I have to ask," she said, "but are you going to join Chad and Jason on the basketball court?"

"Absolutely," Troy replied. He pulled out a whistle on a long red cord from his pocket and twirled it around his finger. "My dad gave me one of his whistles. I'm all set!"

Gabriella laughed. "Okay, Coach Troy Bolton! Those kids are going to be so excited. When they hear that the championship team is going to coach them, they will be so excited!"

"I hope you're right," Troy replied. "And I hope we can do half as good a job as my dad."

Taylor approached Kelsi next. "Kelsi, what would you like to volunteer for?"

"Well, I thought it would be cool to teach a songwriting class," Kelsi replied shyly.

"That's a great idea!" Taylor exclaimed, scribbling notes on her clipboard. "The kids will love that."

Ryan had been walking past and had caught the end of Kelsi and Taylor's conversation.

"What will kids love?" he asked.

"Kelsi has a great idea for the kids at the center. She volunteered to teach them how to write songs!" Taylor told him.

"Hey, that *is* a good idea," Ryan said. "Hmm. Do you mind if I join you?" he asked, looking over at Kelsi. "I do love working on musicals, but it might be really cool to try something new and different."

"Sure!" Kelsi exclaimed. "That would be so much fun."

"Great," Ryan replied. "Taylor, would it be okay if I volunteered for the songwriting class instead?"

"Of course," Taylor told him. "There are plenty of seniors who would love to help out with the musical," she said with a smile.

Sharpay, who had been pretending to be very interested in the cafeteria's lunch special of the day but had really been secretly eavesdropping on Taylor, Ryan, and Kelsi's conversation, walked over to them. "Who wants to write songs, when there's a chance to *sing*?" Sharpay commented in a bored tone. She wrinkled her nose and then grabbed her notebook. "Ryan, don't waste your time on that silly class. You belong on the stage. You know, behind me."

"You mean *next* to you, right?" Ryan added.

"Right, right, whatever," Sharpay said, casually waving her hand. "You know what I mean."

Ryan shook his head. "I know *exactly* what you mean," he muttered. At that moment, Ryan decided that he was going to do something different from what Sharpay wanted. He looked over at Kelsi, who was now waiting in line to pay for her lunch, and he thought about what Sharpay had just told him.

"Ryan, sign me up. I'm sure we can dust off one of our old routines to perform," Sharpay said, interrupting his thoughts. She swung her fuchsia patent-leather bag over her shoulder, and walked away.

Stunned, Taylor looked over at Ryan. "She *does* understand that this is not a performance starring her, right? The kids are going to be the ones onstage?"

Ryan held his finger up to his mouth, signaling Taylor not to say a word until Sharpay was completely out of earshot. He watched as his sister strutted out of the cafeteria. "Hold on," he said. When she was out the door, Ryan turned back to Taylor. He took her clipboard and crossed his name off the musical-theater sheet.

Laughing, Taylor took back her clipboard. "Well, you're going to help her, right?"

"If she wants to run the show," Ryan said, "then far be it from me to stop her."

"Okay," Taylor agreed hesitantly. "I can't wait to see . . . um, I mean, *hear* what you and Kelsi come up with! That's really fantastic that you two are going to work together."

"Well, we'll see what the kids at the center come up with," Ryan said. "I'm sure that Kelsi has some good ideas for the kids, and I'm looking forward to the experience. I love to dance, but writing songs is pretty cool."

"I'll say," Taylor agreed. "Thanks for helping out and for getting Sharpay on board, too." She collected the committee sheets and looked over all the signatures. Most of the senior class had already committed to volunteering! Taylor smiled. She just knew that this senior project was going to be the best one East High had ever seen!

CHAPTER THREE

Troy's red pickup truck clanked and hissed as he pulled into a parking space at the Wellington Community Center. He looked over at Gabriella after he turned off the engine. "Are you ready, coach?" he asked teasingly.

Giggling, Gabriella nodded her head. "I can say the same thing to you!" she joked back, climbing out of the truck. She swung her gym bag over her shoulder. "You have your whistle? Your game plan?"

"Whistle, check," Troy said, twirling it around his finger as he walked toward the front door. "And I got a game plan, right up here," he said, pointing to his forehead. "The guys and I were talking last night about all the drills we're going to show the kids today. We're all set."

As they headed into the community center, Gabriella put her hand on Troy's shoulder. "Well, go easy on them!" she teased. "I don't think these kids have ever had a basketball coach before. They don't know what they are in for with Sergeant Bolton's practice drills!"

Troy laughed. "Oh, I'll be sure to go easy on them," he promised. Then a smile crept across his face. "In the beginning, I mean!" He pushed a lock of hair out of his blue eyes. He lowered his voice and tried to sound like his dad. "Drills are the way to build a team. Teamwork is how games are won."

"You know it!" Chad called, overhearing Troy's comment.

Chad, Zeke, and Jason were waiting for Troy at the entrance to the gym. Like Troy, they were wearing their red-and-white Wildcat warm-up suits. They all looked very official!

"If your dad's practices have taught us anything, it's that if there's no pain, there's no gain!" Chad exclaimed. He turned to Jason and gave him a high five.

"Go Wildcats!" Jason cheered. "We're going to teach those kids how to play the game like pros!"

"*And* have fun," Zeke added. He knocked the basketball out of Chad's hands and started to run down the hallway, with Chad chasing after him.

Just then, a man wearing a baseball cap and a tracksuit walked up to Troy and Gabriella.

"Troy Bolton," the man bellowed. "I'm Mr. Finley. I run the sports program here at the center. We've got a great group of kids. They're really excited that you guys are here to volunteer. I've told them all about you guys."

Troy smiled. "Not as excited as we are, sir. This is going to be a lot of fun."

"It's going to be awesome!" a voice exclaimed from behind them. A young boy with wire-rimmed glasses and shaggy blond hair looked up at Troy. "Are you Troy Bolton? I can't believe that you're here. I've seen you play at East High. You're amazing!"

Troy smiled at the boy. "Thanks, buddy," he said, holding out his hand for a formal hand-shake. "What's your name?"

"I'm Alex Lawson," the boy said, shaking Troy's hand. "And in there are Rosie, Darren, Emma, Peter, Andrew, Evan, and Ben." He pointed inside the gym where the rest of the kids were sitting on the bleachers.

"Looks like a great team," Troy said. "Let's get started, huh? We've got some great drills to show you guys."

Mr. Finley smiled. "You heard Troy," he said to Alex. "Let's get going!"

As everyone headed inside the gym, Troy

glanced over at Gabriella. "Good luck at the pool," he told her. "I'll see you later."

"Have fun, Wildcats!" Gabriella called as she walked down the hall toward the swimming pool. She was so glad that Troy and some of the other Wildcats were going to coach the kids. Having a senior project where everyone was helping out with something that they loved to do was a bonus.

Gabriella was glad that she had decided to volunteer with the swimming program at the center. Mr. Hall, the man in charge of the program, was very excited to have Gabriella work with some of the youngest swimmers. When she had talked to him about volunteering, he had mentioned how he needed the most help with the group of five-year-olds. He explained that some of the children were afraid to put their faces in the water. He thought that some individual attention for some of the kids would help them out. Gabriella knew all about the fear of going underwater. Even though she was now an expert swimmer and a trained lifeguard, she remembered how nervous she had been when she had first started swimming.

As she walked into the locker room, she took a deep breath. She could smell the familiar scent of chlorine from the pool as she put her things in a locker. When she was a kid, she always loved going to the pool. Being in the locker room brought back many old memories of swimming lessons and good times in the water.

I hope this goes well, she thought, heading toward the pool. Swimming was a sport that she loved, and Gabriella hoped that she could pass on that enthusiasm to someone else. As she opened the door to the pool, she saw five little kids sitting along the shallow end. Mr. Hall was in the water, talking to them.

"Today we have a special helper," he said when he saw Gabriella walking toward him. "I'd like everyone to please say hello to Gabriella Montez. She's a fantastic swimmer from East High and is going to be helping us with some of our water skills for the next few weeks."

Gabriella gave a wave and sat down on the edge of the pool next to a little boy. He didn't look over at her as she sat down.

"Hi, everyone," Gabriella said to the group.

Some of the kids waved and said hello, but the little boy next to her didn't say a thing. He kept his head down and just stared at the water. When Mr. Hall asked Gabriella to demonstrate how to blow bubbles in the water, she jumped into the pool and showed the group. But the little boy at the end of the pool still didn't look up.

"Henry James," Mr. Hall said to the boy. "Would you like to try?"

For the first time, Henry raised his eyes. Then he shook his head from side to side very quickly.

"That's okay," Gabriella said, walking over to him. "Maybe we can try together later."

Mr. Hall gave Gabriella a knowing look and then moved on to help another little girl.

Henry must have been one of the boys who

needed the extra attention that Mr. Hall had told her about, Gabriella thought. She hoped Henry would at least look up at her once during the class!.

At the end of the hour-long session, Gabriella had learned all the names of the kids in the class and had helped each of them with some water skills. The only one who would not get in the water was Henry. And he didn't look in Gabriella's direction once!

After the kids had left, Mr. Hall walked over to Gabriella, who had just taken off her swimming goggles. "So Henry doesn't say much, huh?" he commented. He explained that Henry was new to Albuquerque and was painfully shy. "He'll get the hang of swimming," Mr. Hall told her. "I'm sure we'll be able to work with him."

Gabriella hoped that Mr. Hall was right. As she headed out of the center and walked toward Troy's truck in the parking lot, Gabriella vowed that she'd get Henry in the water at least once before the senior project was over. Seeing anyone that shy and afraid made Gabriella want to reach out to help. Having been the new kid so many times, she could totally relate.

"Hey, Gabriella," Troy called. He swooped up behind her and spun her around. "How'd swimming go?"

"It was good," Gabriella said, trying to sound upbeat. But her expression told Troy another story.

"Uh-oh," he said, sensing something was wrong. "What happened?"

Gabriella climbed into the truck and explained to Troy how Henry wouldn't even look in her direction and how he refused to get into the water.

"Seems like you've got your work cut out for you," Troy responded. "Henry doesn't realize how lucky he is to have you as his teacher. I'm sure things will work out."

Settling back against her seat, Gabriella hoped that Troy was right. Now that she had met the kids in the swimming class, she was even more dedicated to helping them learn how to swim.

"How was practice?" she asked, changing the subject. "Show those kids any special Wildcat moves?"

Troy shook his head. "Coaching is hard work!" he exclaimed. "We stuck to some basic drills. Those kids have a ton of energy and enthusiasm. And this little girl Rosie is amazing! She can really play!"

Gabriella loved seeing how excited Troy was about coaching. Touched that Troy already felt so strongly about the Wellington Community Center, Gabriella couldn't stop smiling.

"Hey, guys!" Zeke called out when he saw Gabriella and Troy. "Would you mind tasting this banana smoothie? I just whipped up a new batch and I'd love some taste testers." He reached into the truck to pass them each a cup of his newest concoction. "I was thinking of making these for the kids at the center. They're healthy, and they taste really good, too."

Troy took a sip. "Wow," he said, as he sampled the smoothie. "This is great. The kids are going to love these, Zeke."

"Thanks," Zeke said, grinning. "I've been trying to get this just right. It's a careful balance of fruit and yogurt, you know. I'm going to hand them out tomorrow before practice. You know, pump up the team."

"From what I saw," Taylor said, walking over to her friends, "the kids are very excited about us being here!" She and Chad joined the growing circle around Troy's truck. "I caught the end of the basketball drills and I was really impressed. The kids were really great. And so were you guys. It looked like a good practice!"

"And why wouldn't it be a good practice?" Chad asked teasingly. He puffed out his chest. "You've got the back-to-back state champs coaching! That has to mean something."

"Let's hope," Troy said, putting his key in the ignition.

"How was tutoring?" Gabriella asked Taylor,

leaning out the window to speak to her friend. She hoped that Taylor had had better success than she did.

Taylor walked closer to Gabriella. "There were a few kids there. I was really happy to help." Taylor turned to reach out for one of Zeke's smoothie samples. Then, leaning in closer to Gabriella, she said, "But there was one girl who wouldn't talk to me at all!"

"Oh, I had one of those, too" Gabriella said with a heavy sigh. "This little boy, Henry, wouldn't even look at me! He is so shy, and he wouldn't even get into the pool."

Taylor put her hand on Gabriella's arm. "Well, he will before the end of our senior project," she predicted. "And maybe Sue Corbett, one of the kids in my program, will answer at least one question that I ask her."

"I guess we just have to be patient," Gabriella told her.

"Everyone is saying how great this year's senior project is, Gabriella," Taylor told her.

"You've gotten everyone to come together to work here. It's going to turn out great."

Gabriella was glad that all the seniors were excited about the center and helping the kids there. But she had to wonder, what if she was the only one who wasn't able to help out all the kids in her group? What if Henry never spoke to her? She'd feel like a complete failure as a swimming teacher . . . and she didn't want that to happen, for her sake—or for Henry's. For Gabriella, senior project had officially changed to Project Henry.

CHAPTER FOUR

A little later that day, Sharpay rushed into the theater at the community center. She had to get ready for her stage performance, and she knew that everyone would be awaiting her grand entrance. A star can make the audience wait, she always said. And everyone knew that Sharpay was a star with a capital S.

Backstage, Sharpay wasted no time. She put her bag down and took off her long pink coat to reveal a sequined blue satin outfit. She quickly slipped off her ballet flats and exchanged them for blue satin jazz shoes, then took out a feathered hat from her tote bag. She looked in the mirror and smiled. So what if Ryan wasn't going to perform with her. She didn't need him!

Taking a deep breath, she looked into the mirror and smiled. Then she did a few quick breathing exercises, and fluttered her fingers and hands to warm up. Before going onstage, she had a few rituals that she always had to do to prepare. She exhaled one last time, and then she proudly waltzed out to the center of the stage.

Lights? Music? Applause?

What is going on here? Sharpay wondered as she stood in the silent darkness.

She held her pose for a moment longer. Perhaps there was a technical difficulty, she thought. As a professional, she knew that she had to hold her pose until the problem was fixed. At any moment her music would fill the auditorium, and then she could begin. She remained as still as a mannequin with her arms held up high above her head and her feet perfectly turned out. She held her gaze straight ahead and fought to keep her focus. Any moment now, she thought. Any moment and she'd be ready to sing and dance her heart out.

Silence.

Hmmm, she thought. What is going on here?

Finally, Sharpay lost her patience. She broke her pose and stomped her foot on the stage. Sticking her hip out, she crossed her arms over her chest.

"Ryan!" she cried into the darkness. He was probably responsible for this whole mess, she thought. She paced the length of the stage, then stopped and stomped her foot several times. "Where's my cue?" she shouted.

Just then, the lights came on, and an older woman and a group of children walked into the auditorium.

"You must be Sharpay," the woman said. "I'm Miss Hewson. I was just keeping an eye on the kids until you arrived. They're really excited that you're here."

"Well, of *course* they are," Sharpay huffed. "I can sing, dance, and act—I'm what performers call a 'triple threat.'"

Miss Hewson raised an eyebrow. "Well, that's great," she said dryly. "I'll leave you with the kids now so you can pass along your vast knowledge," she added as she headed out of the auditorium.

"Well, hello everyone," Sharpay said haughtily. She looked around the vacant stage. "Um, where is the set?" Sharpay gasped, turning around in a circle. "I *specifically* told Ryan all the details of the act. He said that he wasn't going to join me, which is fine, because I can handle a solo, but this is ridiculous. . . ."

As Sharpay rambled on, she failed to realize that her audience of kids was standing quietly in the first few rows, staring at her with their mouths open.

"Um, excuse me," a little girl with a ponytail finally said. She bravely inched closer to Sharpay. "I think we're a little confused."

Sharpay stopped talking and spun around on her heel to stare at the girl. *"Confused?"* she asked.

"Well, if it helps," the girl continued cautiously, "we weren't expecting a whole show."

"You weren't?" Sharpay asked, shocked.

"Actually, we were expecting to be *in* a show, not to watch one," the girl explained. She walked over to Sharpay and extended her hand. "I'm Rosie Reynolds," she said.

Sharpay looked at the girl carefully, taking in her athletic shorts, sweatshirt, and high-top sneakers. "You didn't come here to see a performance?" Sharpay asked, still stunned. "Isn't this the Wellington Community Center *show*?"

"Well, not yet," Rosie corrected her. She dropped her hand down to her side when Sharpay didn't reach out to shake it. "The idea was that we could use this theater for something other than meetings and rainy-day activities. We'd love to put on a show." She gestured toward the group of kids, now all sitting down in the seats. "We signed up to be *in* a show."

Looking at the group of kids in front of her, Sharpay wrinkled her nose and scratched her head. In her head, she replayed the last few conversations with Ryan. It was entirely possible that she had not listened very carefully when Ryan had told her about today. And maybe she hadn't been too nice about his wanting to do that songwriting thing with Kelsi, but she was pretty sure that she had signed up to be *in* a show for the center. Wasn't that what he had said in the cafeteria when she was rushing off? Didn't Taylor ask her to help out by performing? It was for the senior project, that much she was sure of. But where was everyone else?

"Ryan?" Sharpay called. She looked around the stage. "All right, very funny. You can come out now."

Rosie and her friends watched as Sharpay raced around the stage peeking behind curtains and old boxes.

"Is anyone else from East High here?" Sharpay asked.

"Well, we just had a great basketball practice with the varsity team," Rosie said, stepping closer. "Those guys were amazing! We had so much fun with them. I think we have a chance to beat the team from the Southside Center. The game is in a few weeks."

Sharpay sighed and looked away. Rosie grabbed her books, as two sisters, Hannah and Carly Rosen, pulled their backpacks on over their shoulders.

"It was a good idea, Rosie," Hannah said. "But I guess not enough seniors came to help out. So much for my shot at being a big star onstage."

"She's definitely not going to teach us anything," Carly added, looking over at Sharpay. "She probably doesn't know anything about putting on a show. Let's go."

Holding her hand up, Sharpay called out to the two little girls walking away up the aisle. She didn't need all of East High to teach these kids about musical theater. Wasn't she co-president of the Drama Club? Wasn't she the *real* star of the East High musicals? She wasn't sure what sort of joke Ryan was playing on her, but she did not find it funny. If these kids wanted to put on a musical, then she was going to show them how to make that happen.

"Here's what we're going to do," Sharpay announced. "I'm going to teach you a song that you can perform onstage."

Hannah turned around. "Carly, did you *hear* that?" she asked her sister. "She *is* going to teach us! See, we *will* be able to put on a show like the kids at East High!"

"You'd better believe it!" Sharpay exclaimed. She grinned at her new students. "This show is going to be the best show you've ever seen. Just you guys wait and see!"

* * *

An hour later, in the community center's parking lot, Sharpay leaned against her pink convertible. There was no way that she was going to let Ryan know how embarrassed she had been on that stage. She had to turn this situation around immediately. Wiping a smudge of dirt off the door, she settled back against the car and waited.

When she saw Ryan walk out of the center chatting with Kelsi, she stood up straighter and tossed her hair back. She flashed Ryan a huge smile and called to him sweetly, "Hi, Ryan!" She raised her arm and waved her hand dramatically. "Oh, Ryan—over here!"

Ryan was hesitant to walk over. He knew that it probably hadn't been very nice of him to neglect to tell Sharpay that he wouldn't be volunteering with her, and that she would not be the star of a musical. But for once he didn't want to listen to his sister boss him around. As he walked toward her car, he became anxious.

Sharpay was grinning as if she had just won an award, not pouting and stomping her foot as he would have expected.

"Hey, Sharpay!" he called out nervously. He glanced over at Kelsi. She looked just as surprised to see Sharpay so giddy and happy.

"Hi, guys," Sharpay sang out. "Silly me, there was no show . . . yet." She grinned. "But I'm actually going to direct the kids *in* a show. How fabulous is that? Me, a director! It's going to be the best show *ever*!"

Ryan caught Kelsi's eye. He was not sure what Sharpay was up to, but he had a feeling their senior project was about to take a very different turn from the one he had expected.

Sharpay jumped into her car. "Ryan, I need to run some errands before I head home. Surely Kelsi can drive you home, right?" she asked. "Toodles!" she called over her shoulder.

As she drove away, Sharpay vowed that she'd show the kids at the Wellington Community Center a show that they'd never forget. After all, Sharpay thought, I have *tons* of experience onstage. What can be so different? Plus, she thought smugly, I *never* back away from a challenge!

CHAPTER FIVE

Zeke clapped his hands together as he tasted his latest batch of banana smoothies. He went to the community center immediately after school so he could get right to work on his newest recipes. He was sure that Mr. Lowell, the head cook who worked at the center, would approve of the new beverage—and of his zucchini muffins, which were cooling in their tins on the counter.

"How's it going?" Mr. Lowell said pleasantly as he entered the kitchen. He put his hands on his hips and chuckled. "Something smells really good in here." He sniffed the air, walked around the kitchen, and went over to Zeke and peered over his shoulder. "What are you up to, master baker?"

Smiling, Zeke showed him the trays of cooling muffins. "I tried out a new recipe," he told him. "They're zucchini muffins. I looked through the recipes that you gave me yesterday to experiment with and I picked this one."

Baking was Zeke's passion, and making nutritious treats for the kids at the center had proven to be really fun for him. When Gabriella told Mr. Lowell that Zeke loved to bake, the head cook soon called upon him to spend some time in the community center's kitchen. "I'm going to give these to the kids after basketball practice today," Zeke said. "They're probably going to be starving after all those drills that the Wildcats are making them practice this afternoon."

"Well, these look fantastic!" Mr. Lowell exclaimed. He brushed his hands on his apron as he peered into the trays cooling on the rack. "May I try one?"

Zeke handed him a muffin and waited for his response. The cook's face instantly gave Zeke his review.

"These are great!" he exclaimed. "Well done!"

Reaching for the large boxes on the shelf, Zeke started to pack up the muffins. "Thanks," he said proudly. "I really appreciate having the opportunity to try out some new recipes. Try the smoothie, too. My friends tasted it yesterday and thought it was really good." He poured Mr. Lowell a cup.

"Now, that's nutritious *and* delicious!" Mr. Lowell said enthusiastically.

Laughing, Zeke reached out to shake the cook's hand. "Really? I take that as a huge compliment. Thanks so much!"

"You should," Mr. Lowell said. "Thanks again, Zeke. We all appreciate what East High is doing for the center. There's a new energy here, and it's fantastic. And I know for sure that the kids on the basketball team are excited about the big game coming up."

"We're excited, too," Zeke said. "There's a lot of raw talent on the team. We just have to get them all to work together."

"You guys will do it. I'm sure of it," Mr. Lowell said. "I have to run to a meeting, but I'll see you later. And again, thank you," he added with a smile.

As Mr. Lowell walked out of the kitchen, Zeke finished packing up the food. All the muffins were neatly stored in boxes, and he had two big containers full of smoothies. He was all set for the after-practice snack. Practice would be ending soon, and he'd be prepared. Carefully, he picked up the containers by their handles, grasped the stack of boxes under his arms, and pushed open the door with his back to head down to the gymnasium. But just as he walked out the door, he lost his balance and slipped on the slick tiled floor in the hallway!

"Whoa!" Zeke yelled, trying not to drop any of the boxes or the containers.

Luckily, Ryan and Kelsi were in a room right across the hall, huddled around Kelsi's portable piano, working on a song. They sprang up quickly and ran out to the hall when they heard Zeke yell.

Ryan, always quick on his feet, reached Zeke first. "Hey, are you okay?"

"Yeah," Zeke said, a little embarrassed. "I'm okay." He piled up the boxes and then stood up. "Pretty graceful, huh?" he joked.

"Actually, that was incredibly graceful," Kelsi commented. "And you managed to save whatever you were carrying."

"I made some banana smoothies and zucchini muffins for the center's basketball team," Zeke told them. "I'm trying to expand my recipes and include some healthy snacks for the kids. Do you want to try a muffin?"

"Definitely, thanks," Ryan told him. He lifted the top off of one of the boxes.

"Mmmm," Kelsi said as she peered into the box. "Zeke, those look amazing." She took a bite and smiled. "And they taste just as good as they look."

Blushing, Zeke lowered his head. "They are pretty good, huh?" he said sheepishly. "I was thinking of not telling the kids that they have zucchini in them . . . that they're just some power snacks to help their game."

Kelsi laughed. "That's a good idea," she said. "But I don't think anyone is going to complain. These are delicious."

"We can help you carry these to the gym," Ryan offered. "We just finished working on a new song."

"Thanks," Zeke said, happy for the extra pair of hands. "But wait, a songwriting class? I thought that you guys were working on the show with Sharpay." Zeke couldn't help but smile when he said Sharpay's name. Everyone at East High knew that Zeke liked Sharpay.

Ryan took a bite of his muffin and shook his

head. "No, Kelsi and I are helping a group of kids with their own music," he said. "There are some very talented kids here. It's been very cool."

Grabbing a box, Kelsi agreed with Ryan. "I can't believe what we accomplished in one session. I was blown away by some of their lyrics. The songs are so heartfelt, and really good."

"But what about the show?" Zeke asked. He scratched his head, thinking about what he had heard earlier that day. "Didn't I hear Sharpay talking about some big show this morning during homeroom?"

Turning around to face Zeke, Ryan nodded his head up and down. "Oh, yes," he said. "I think everyone heard her talking about 'The Show.' Apparently, she has taken quite well to the role of director." Ryan pushed his hair out of his eyes as he walked along carrying the muffin boxes. "I thought Sharpay would be really mad about directing the show without being *in* the show," he said curiously. "But I guess I was wrong."

"Maybe all that time she spends with Ms. Darbus has rubbed off on her," Kelsi commented.

"I really didn't think that she'd stay with it," Ryan said. "But she says that she really likes directing and that the kids adore her."

Zeke reached out and pulled the gym door open. "Well, I don't doubt that for one minute," Zeke said. "Who wouldn't want to rehearse with Sharpay?"

In the gym, there were ten kids running the length of the court as Troy and Chad blew their whistles and coached the kids.

"Break time!" Zeke called as he walked in. "I've got some snacks to power up your game!"

Instantly, all the players came running over. Ryan put the boxes down, and Zeke started pouring smoothies into plastic cups.

"Thanks, guys," Zeke said to Ryan and Kelsi. "I appreciate the help."

"Anytime," Ryan said.

Zeke stood back and enjoyed watching the kids

devour the snacks that he had prepared. He glanced at his watch. Maybe he'd drop by the theater and check in on Sharpay's show. He was sure that the rehearsals were going well and that the performance would be amazing. From what Sharpay had said earlier that day, the show was bound to be one of the shining moments of the senior project!

In the theater, Sharpay was trying to get her group to focus. "Everyone!" Sharpay shouted. "Attention, please! You have to listen to the beat!" She sighed and looked at the line of girls in front of her. She turned on her heel and faced the front of the stage, tossing her hair over to one side. This was proving to be much harder than she had originally thought it would be. "Let's start again at the beginning of the song," she said, trying to be patient. She pointed her finger at the boy sitting by the tape player at the edge of the stage. "Hit it, Max!"

The music began and Sharpay struck a pose. She looked behind her to see if the girls were in position. Hannah, Carly, and three other girls stood at attention, their eyes wide. They were holding the same pose as Sharpay.

"A five, six, seven, eight!" Sharpay yelled as she twirled to the left. She then twirled back to the right and launched into her routine.

Max Crawford lowered his head in his hands, covering his eyes. Rehearsal was *not* going well. Hannah and Carly kept bumping into each other. And the other girls were about three steps behind Sharpay. This was about the tenth time they had run through this number, and still no one onstage was any closer to learning Sharpay's routine. Max hit the STOP button and shook his head in despair. "Nope," he said when Sharpay looked down at him. "No one is following you."

"Can we try it again?" Hannah asked hopefully. She was not willing to give up. But from the expression on Sharpay's face it looked as if she was about to walk out.

"Can you just do the dance again really, really

slowly?" Carly asked. "I keep getting confused about the steps."

Sharpay looked around at the faces staring at her. Sharpay's own expression softened when she saw their disappointed faces. How did Ryan do this choreography thing? In all the shows they had done together, she had never really appreciated the dances that he had taught the cast. Everyone always got the steps when Ryan taught them. Even Jason and Zeke were able to learn the routines when Ryan showed them! What was she doing wrong?

"I'll do the number again, and you can watch," Sharpay said calmly. She cued Max, and the music started.

"Watching you isn't going to help us," Hannah complained. "We all know that *you* know the routine."

Sharpay stared at the little girl glaring at her. While Sharpay loved being the center of attention and having people stare at her, the looks that she was getting now were *not* the kind that she was used to. And she didn't like it at all.

"Okay, okay," Sharpay said, trying to remain patient. She took a deep breath. "Why don't you try taking it from the top? I'll watch." She grabbed her water bottle and sat down on the edge of the stage.

Max hit the PLAY button once again, and Sharpay clapped her hands. "A five, six, seven, eight!"

At that moment, Zeke peeked his head inside the theater. He walked in and sat down in one of the seats. But the chaos on stage was not what he expected to see. Ms. Darbus never ran a rehearsal quite like that! He scanned the room for Sharpay and was surprised to see her standing by herself at the front of the stage, looking helpless.

What is going on here? he wondered. When Sharpay was talking about the show in homeroom that morning, she had never mentioned that no one was actually able to do any of the dance steps! Watching the scene unfold onstage, Zeke realized that maybe Sharpay was afraid to admit she needed help in directing the musical. A *lot* of help.

Max got up from his position by the sound system to get a drink from the water fountain. On his way up the aisle, he passed Zeke.

"How's it going?" Zeke asked him.

Max shrugged. "Not that great. No one can keep up with Sharpay. The show is next week. I'm not sure how this show is going to happen." He shook his head sadly and headed out the door.

Zeke watched Max walk into the hallway with his shoulders slumped. Onstage, the girls were trying to do the dance, but none of them were doing the same steps at the same time. One girl with blond hair kept putting her arms out in front of the others, trying to stay center stage the whole time. The scene was not pretty.

Quietly, Zeke snuck out of the theater without Sharpay spotting him. Poor Sharpay, he thought.

She is so proud that she doesn't want to ask for help. But he knew that she needed reinforcements. If he had learned anything about being in a show over the last year, it was that it took a whole cast to make a performance shine.

This is going to take an all-star team, Zeke thought as he walked out. And I know just the Wildcats to ask for help.

CHAPTER SIX

The next day, before the homeroom bell rang, Zeke scanned the hallways for Ryan. He finally found him at his locker, rummaging through a pile of books. Zeke glanced around to see if Sharpay was nearby, but she was nowhere to be found. Zeke took this as a good time to talk to Ryan about Sharpay's rehearsal the day before.

"Hey, Ryan," Zeke called. "Can I talk to you for a second?"

Ryan wasn't sure what Zeke wanted. But one

look at Zeke's expression and he could tell that it was serious. "Sure," he said, shutting his locker door. "What's going on?"

"Well, it's kind of what is *not* going on," Zeke told him. He checked up and down the hall to make sure that Sharpay still wasn't anywhere nearby. "I dropped by Sharpay's rehearsal yesterday. Whatever rehearsal she has been describing, it is not what is really going on. Her show is in trouble. I'm no theater expert, but none of the kids were following her and they all looked really confused."

"Huh. Well, that's interesting," Ryan commented casually. He started walking to class.

"Wait!" Zeke called after him. "Ryan, I think she really needs your help."

Ryan stopped walking and looked at Zeke. "If she wants my help, she'll have to ask. She's been telling everyone how she can do this all by herself, and now she can." He walked into homeroom, leaving Zeke standing by himself in the hallway.

The bell rang and Zeke hurried off to homeroom. Just perfect, he thought. Not only had he not gotten help for Sharpay, he was now late for homeroom. He'd have to come up with another idea.

As he raced down the empty hallway, Zeke thought about what Max had said at the theater. He had looked so disappointed! The kids deserved to have a good show. As he slid into his seat in Ms. Darbus's homeroom class, he knew that he had to try harder to recruit helpers.

"You're late, Mr. Baylor," Ms. Darbus said disapprovingly. She stood next to her desk, peering over her glasses. "One more tardy and I'll see you in detention."

"Sorry, Ms. Darbus," Zeke said sincerely. He slumped down in his seat. Gabriella turned around to give him a sympathetic look. Suddenly Zeke had an idea.

That's it! Zeke thought. If he could get Gabriella to help him out, *she* would be able to convince Ryan! Saying no to Gabriella was hard to do. She had a way of getting people to listen to her. Appealing to Gabriella would be easy, he mused. She really wanted the senior project to go well, and besides, she also loved musicals. She'd definitely understand. He hoped that he could convince her to talk to Ryan. At the moment, Gabriella was his only shot.

The homeroom bell rang again, calling all the students to their first period. Zeke only had a couple of minutes to talk to Gabriella. Grabbing his books, he rushed out of class to catch up with her. He came up behind her and Troy, surprising them. He told them quickly about what he had seen at the center the day before. Just as he had thought, Gabriella was very sympathetic and willing to help.

"Wow," Gabriella said after hearing Zeke's report. "We need to help those kids. Funny, I thought Ryan was supposed to be there, too. Didn't he sign up to help out?"

Zeke shook his head. "Ryan decided to volunteer for a songwriting class with Kelsi.

And now he doesn't want to help Sharpay unless she asks, and I'm not sure how to make that happen."

Troy and Gabriella shared a knowing look.

"I'll talk to everyone," Gabriella offered. "The show is an important part of the senior project." As she reached her classroom, she turned to face Zeke. "Thanks for letting me know."

"You bet," Zeke said. "I'm just trying to help out. I know that Sharpay is just too proud to ask for help."

"You're definitely right about that," Gabriella replied. "But putting on a show is not a one-person job. It takes teamwork."

Zeke thanked Gabriella and raced off to arrive at class just moments before the second bell rang. Now he had to hope that Gabriella could change Ryan's mind and get the rest of the Wildcats to help out, too.

At the community center later that afternoon, Gabriella sat at the edge of the pool. She was sitting next to Henry as Mr. Hall talked to the students about using kickboards. He was standing in the shallow end of the pool with the other students. Henry and Gabriella were the only ones who weren't participating in the lesson.

It was the third day of swim class, and Henry still had not said one word to Gabriella—and had not yet gotten in the water. At this point, she just wanted him to look up and smile at her. Maybe getting in the water would come later.

"Hey, Henry," Gabriella said. "Do you want to hold on to my hand?" She slid into the water and extended her hand to him. "Come on," she coaxed him. "I promise that I won't let go."

Henry shook his head no. He pulled his legs out of the water and up to his chest, hugging them close. He was now keeping a safe distance from the pool.

Gabriella didn't want to give up. She slowly moved toward him. "Look, I know that you're scared. But all you have to do is stand in the pool.

The water will only reach up to here on you." She held up her hand to show Henry that the water would reach his waist.

The expression on Henry's face didn't change. He just looked down nervously.

Mr. Hall looked over toward Gabriella and smiled. He knew that she was trying her best. He reached out and handed her a blue kickboard.

"Henry, I'll give this to Gabriella to hold for you in case you change your mind," he said encouragingly, heading over to them. He smiled at Gabriella and then waded back to the other students, who were in the center of the pool.

Gabriella tried another approach. She hopped up on the side of the pool and sat next to Henry. "Do you like animals?" she asked.

Henry shrugged. He pulled his knees tighter to his chest.

Taking his shrugging as a positive sign, Gabriella continued. At least he was listening to what she had to say. She went on. "Well, how about dogs? Do you like dogs?"

This time Henry nodded yes, even though he still wouldn't look up at her.

"Well, did you know that dogs are great swimmers?" Gabriella asked him. "We can pretend that you are a dog learning to swim. Does that sound like fun?"

A smile started to spread across Henry's face. "I have a dog named Rufus," he said shyly.

"Does Rufus like to swim?" Gabriella asked gently.

"Sometimes," Henry said. "When we go to the lake in the summer, he likes to splash around."

Smiling, Gabriella knew that she was making progress. "How about we pretend that you're Rufus now?" She reached out her hand once again, and this time, Henry took it. Very slowly, Henry scooted closer and closer to the pool's edge. Finally, he slowly slid down into the water.

Mr. Hall glanced over at Gabriella and nodded approvingly. He was impressed that Gabriella had stayed with Henry so long, working with him so patiently.

"Good work, Henry!" Gabriella cheered. She couldn't help but melt when Henry's big blue eyes gazed up at her. She'd persuaded Henry to get in the water! He wasn't swimming yet, but this was definitely progress.

When the swimming session was over, Gabriella pulled on her sweats and headed out to the parking lot, where she was meeting up with Troy, Chad, and Taylor. Taylor was already standing by Troy's truck when Gabriella walked up to them.

"I just got these samples from the printer," Taylor told her. She held up a bright red box. "These are the cards for our senior-notes. What do you think?" She pulled one of the cards out of the box to show her. It was a white note card with the image of a roaring Wildcat at the top. She looked at the note and grinned. "Pretty cool, huh?" she said.

Gabriella nodded in agreement and took the card from her friend.

"This year we're going to make sure that we sell tons of senior notes," Taylor informed her. "This is one of the last fundraisers that the seniors are going to do. I want to make sure that every Wildcat participates."

"These look fantastic!" Gabriella replied enthusiastically. She was already thinking about what she would write to Troy on his senior note. The year was going by so quickly! There were so many moments to treasure, and so many special ones that she and Troy had shared together.

"We'll start selling these next week," Taylor said, interrupting Gabriella's thoughts. She put the note back in the box. Then she looked up at Gabriella and grinned. She was waiting to tell her the best part about the notes. "Part of the money that we raise is going to be donated to the community center," she said, beaming. "Principal Matsui just approved my request this afternoon. I thought that would be a really nice way to add to our senior project."

Gabriella smiled. "That's great news, Taylor,"

she said. "The center could certainly use some extra funds."

"And Ryan has agreed to deliver the notes dressed as the Wildcat mascot!" Taylor exclaimed happily. "How great to have Wylie Wildcat deliver the notes!"

"Perfect," Gabriella agreed. She was thrilled that everyone had gotten so involved with the senior project, and now with extra money there could be more programming for the kids at the center. "How were things with Sue today? Did she talk to you?"

Taylor shrugged. "I'm really trying, but she doesn't want to talk to me at all! Seriously, I have tried everything. Maybe she just doesn't like me."

Shaking her head, Gabriella gave Taylor a playful shove. "Come on," she said. "She'll warm up. You have to give her time. And find something that she relates to. Today I got Henry in the water! I mentioned that dogs like to swim, and that really helped him. I think he even enjoyed class today!"

"Wow," Taylor said. "That's awesome!"

Gabriella leaned against Troy's truck, gazing at the sun, which was beginning to set. "It's definitely a start. I still have to get him to put his face in the water. But I was really proud of him today."

Taylor looked over toward the community center's doors, and then glanced at her watch. "Where are those Wildcats? I'm starving! I thought that we were going to get a snack. But it's going to be more like dinner if they don't hurry up."

"They are taking these basketball practices very seriously," Gabriella told her. "I think it's really nice how the whole team is pitching in to help."

"What's our name? Wildcats!" Taylor shouted. Then she giggled. "Hey, do I sound like Chad or what?"

Gabriella nodded. "You do!" Then she remembered what she wanted to talk to Taylor about. "So I heard from Zeke that Sharpay is having a problem with the musical," she said.

"What kind of problem?" Taylor asked. "I heard Sharpay gloating yesterday, saying how terrific the show is going to be."

"I think she may be exaggerating. She needs a little help," Gabriella said gently.

Taylor narrowed her eyes. "She growled at me when I was asking for volunteers. And she promised that she would do this. She's the one who wanted to do the show. And she's been walking around gloating about her big debut as a director."

Realizing that she had to act fast, Gabriella tried to sway her friend. "Teamwork, remember? Come on, Taylor. Where's your compassion? Your sense of community? It's not just Sharpay who needs our help. This is for the senior project, for the center."

Taylor sighed and seemed to relent. "Okay, I'll help," she said when she saw Gabriella's face. "But *not* to help Sharpay. This is for the kids at the center, for the senior project."

"Thanks, Taylor," Gabriella said gratefully. She noticed the door to the community center swing open. "Here come the Wildcats," she said, pointing to the door.

"I'm so hungry," Taylor said again. "Let's get them moving."

"Sounds good to me," Gabriella replied. She was relieved that Taylor had agreed to help out with the musical. Now that Gabriella had one Wildcat on board, she would have to talk to the others about helping out with the show. She hoped that she'd be able to convince them all that helping Sharpay was really about helping the center and helping all the kids who wanted to be in a musical. It was about the senior project— about making sure that it would be something the Wildcats would always remember.

CHAPTER SEVEN

Sharpay flipped on the light switch in her backstage dressing room. So much of her life at East High had been about the stage and this dressing room. Whenever she felt sad, she came here to think. This was the place where she felt the most comfortable, and the room was filled with memories from shows past. All her flashy costumes hung on the rack. She loved this room! She sat down at the mirror and stared at her reflection.

"You are a star, Sharpay Evans," she said to her reflection in the mirror. "You can be a director, too." She was trying to psych herself up for the rehearsal at the community center in a couple of hours. She still couldn't bring herself to ask Ryan for help. Asking him would mean that she was a failure, and Sharpay Evans would never admit that. She applied a bit more lip gloss to her pouty lips. Just then there was a gentle knock on the door.

"May I come in?" Ms. Darbus asked, poking her head inside the dressing room. "I thought that I might find you here."

Sharpay was never so happy to see Ms. Darbus. She was exactly the person who could help. If anyone knew about directing, it was Ms. Darbus.

"Yes, please," Sharpay said graciously, jumping up out of her seat. She cleared off a stool for Ms. Darbus to sit down on, pushing a pink boa and a sequined top to the floor.

Ms. Darbus looked over at Sharpay. "How is

everything going?" She regarded her student with a concerned expression. "You don't seem quite yourself these days. Tell me, is there something bothering you?"

Looking over at her teacher, Sharpay felt as if she might burst. She hated to admit it, but she really needed help directing the musical at the center.

"Well, actually—" Sharpay began to say, but then stopped. How could she admit to Ms. Darbus that she was a failure as a director? She decided to try another tactic. She *was* an actress, after all! "I was wondering if you'd like to come see what's going on at the Wellington Community Center theater."

"Hmm," Ms. Darbus said, with her eyebrows raised. She pushed her glasses up on her nose. "Isn't that the show you're putting together for the senior project?"

"Yes!" Sharpay exclaimed. "How did you know?" She tossed her head to the side. She'd have to play this *very* carefully if she were going to get Ms. Darbus to help her direct the show. "To be honest, I could really use some help. What I need is someone with a tremendous amount of experience. Someone who has the knowledge and the talent to direct a group of talented kids. I just don't have that," she admitted.

Ms. Darbus looked at Sharpay sympathetically. "I see," she said. She leaned forward on the stool. "You have found that performing and directing are really very different, aren't they?"

Sharpay's smile quickly faded from her face. She put her head in her hands. "They really are," Sharpay replied. "But it's all Ryan's fault," she complained. "I thought I was signing up to star in a show for the kids at the center. I didn't realize that I would be . . ." A horrified looked crossed Sharpay's face. "That I'd be . . . a director!" she finally spat out. "And all by myself!" Suddenly she burst into tears.

Ms. Darbus put a hand on Sharpay's shoulder. "Being a director is one of the most creative and energizing roles in the theater," she explained. "You will excel at the role, just as you perfect every role that you have ever played here on the stage at East High."

Sharpay lifted her head, grabbed a tissue, and blew her nose. Sitting up straighter, she took a deep breath. Sharpay felt a little better now that she had finally been able to say what was on her mind. "You really think I can do this?" she asked softly.

"Yes, but you need to remember something," her teacher warned. She peered at her through her large glasses.

"What's that?" Sharpay asked. She leaned closer to Ms. Darbus. She hoped that her teacher was about to reveal to her the deepest secret of directing. Or maybe Ms. Darbus was going to volunteer to pitch in. It was so hard getting all those kids to follow directions! More help, especially from Ms. Darbus, would be welcome. "Will you help me?" Sharpay asked hopefully.

"Oh, Sharpay," Ms. Darbus replied, clucking

her tongue. "This is not my senior project. You need to figure out how to solve this problem."

Sharpay looked down sadly. She grabbed a powderpuff off the table and blotted her face. "But I'm an actor, not a director," she said despondently. "What if I'm terrible?"

"You know, many directors have been, at one time, actors," Ms. Darbus explained. She paused and caught a glimpse of her reflection in the mirror. She touched a hand to her hair to fix a stray strand out of place. "Including yours truly."

Turning in her seat, Sharpay faced Ms. Darbus. "Really?"

Ms. Darbus got off the stool and reached for one of Sharpay's boas. She wrapped it around her neck and stood perfectly still. "Yes, my dear," she said in an English accent. "I once loved being center stage—and I still do!" She took another moment to admire herself in the mirror, flipping the boa around her neck again. "Oh, yes," she said, "I still act on the stage. You can never stop once you've been bitten by the acting bug!"

"Ms. Darbus!" Sharpay gasped. "I didn't know that you still performed."

"Acting is a fierce desire that does not end," her teacher told her. "And in fact, I think you will find that *teaching* the dramatic arts is often the most rewarding work." She twirled around with her arms stretched wide and then took a deep bow. "And no one is saying that you are not still a star." She winked and hung up the boa on a hook on the wall.

"The point is that I am a total failure as a director," Sharpay admitted. She looked up at Ms. Darbus, full of hope. "Please, can you help me?"

Ms. Darbus reached for the doorknob, and gave Sharpay a warm smile. "A good director knows how to staff a production. A show, no matter how small, needs a choreographer, a musical director, and a stage manager. These are the essentials to a smooth performance. But the director has to provide the total vision for the show." With these parting words, Ms. Darbus walked out of the dressing room.

Sharpay turned back to the mirror, and stared at herself. "A vision, huh?" she wondered aloud. She hoped that she would realize the vision soon. She was due at the Wellington Community Center theater in a little while.

Gabriella found Ryan and Kelsi in the music room during their free period. Kelsi was playing a soft melody on the piano and Ryan was standing next to her, shuffling through some papers.

"I love this," Kelsi said as she played the song. She was reading from handwritten sheet music. "James Connelly's song is really good! I can't believe that this is the first song he's ever written. He's amazing."

"That song does sound incredible!" Gabriella exclaimed, coming up behind Kelsi. "Is James one of the kids from your songwriting class at the center?"

Kelsi stopped playing and gathered up the music in front of her. "Yeah," she replied. "Isn't his song great? Ryan and I have met a bunch of really talented kids." She glanced at Ryan over the rims of her glasses. "I'm so glad that we decided to do this workshop."

"Me, too," Ryan said. He couldn't help but blush a little.

"Awesome, guys. Hey, maybe you would be interested in helping out with the musical, too?" Gabriella asked gently.

"Otherwise known as 'The Sharpay Show'?" Ryan corrected her. He pulled his hat down lower to shade his eyes. "No, thanks." He shifted his attention back to the pile of handwritten sheet music Kelsi had set down beside the piano.

Gabriella knew that she had to change their minds. Their senior project needed this musical. The kids at the center needed this show, too! And the musical *really* needed Ryan and Kelsi's help.

"You know, these kids are really looking forward to putting on a special show," she said quietly. She moved closer to Ryan and Kelsi.

"And they will," Ryan said. "Sharpay will

figure something out. It's her show, after all."

Gabriella gave Ryan a serious look. "Zeke stopped in at a rehearsal yesterday," Gabriella said. She lowered her voice. "I don't think things are going as well as Sharpay would like us to think."

Ryan suddenly looked somber. "I think he tried to tell me, but I just wasn't in the mood to listen," he said quietly. His expression softened. "Wow, Sharpay had me fooled. She kept saying everything was going well. I guess that she's a better actress than I have given her credit for. I really believed her."

Gabriella put her hand on Ryan's shoulder. "She needs our help," she told him. "And most of all, she needs you."

"We're all signing on to help," Troy said as he walked into the room. "We're all here to get assignments for after basketball practice today."

Little did Gabriella know that Zeke had mentioned the musical to Troy, who had told the rest of the Wildcats. They were all eager to help out.

Behind Troy, a stream of Wildcats filed into the room. Chad, Jason, Zeke, Taylor, and Martha surrounded the piano, ready to lend a hand to the production. Seeing all her friends rally to help warmed Gabriella's heart and made her smile.

We're ready to do whatever we can to help!" Martha cheered.

"Absolutely," Jason agreed. "Count us in."

"I think I can take time out of my busy baking schedule to help," Zeke teased.

Troy grabbed Gabriella's hand and gave it a squeeze. Then he faced Kelsi and Ryan. "You're the music makers," he said. "Let's make some music!"

Kelsi couldn't believe it. She looked at all the smiling faces around her. "Have all of you guys ever actually *been* in the East High music room before?" she asked, laughing.

"I haven't," Chad admitted. "But it is kind of nice in here," he added, walking around and checking out all the music stands and chairs. He bounced his basketball a few times and then headed back to the piano.

"So," Gabriella said, looking over at Kelsi and Ryan. "What do you say?" She held her breath as she waited for their response.

"I can't believe that all of you are begging me to do a musical!" Ryan exclaimed. A huge grin was on his face. He took off his hat and tossed it down on the piano. "I'm in!" he announced.

Everyone in the room cheered.

"Kelsi?" Gabriella asked. "We can't have a musical without a musical director. What do you say?"

Kelsi looked down at the piano keys and then back up at Gabriella. "I'll do it," she said. "But I'd like to ask permission to use some of the songs that the kids have written in our class. We have some great songs, and if we use them, the show will *really* be theirs."

"That's an awesome idea!" Gabriella gushed. She was so relieved. "Now all we have to do is tell Sharpay," she said. She wasn't sure how Sharpay would handle everyone showing up at the theater, but she hoped that she would be happy to see them all. If what Zeke said was true, Sharpay had to be open to getting everyone to pitch in. After all, the show must go on!

CHAPTER EIGHT

By the time the Wildcats arrived at the Wellington Community Center that afternoon it had started to rain, but the weather couldn't keep their spirits down. They all reported to the center for their activities. The boys went to the gym, Ryan and Kelsi went to their song-writing class, and Gabriella headed to the pool. Taylor, Martha, and a few others went to the study room and to the game room. Gabriella had arranged for everyone to meet at the theater after their activities were over. She hoped that Sharpay would be happy to see them all there, ready to do whatever they could to help. This musical needed teamwork, and Gabriella was going to bring the best team she knew.

As Taylor sat in her seat at a small table in the study room, she anxiously checked her watch. She hoped that Sue Corbett, the shy girl in her group, would be arriving soon. Today, Taylor was hoping that the little girl would come out of her shell and maybe, just maybe, talk to her.

Martha and a few other Wildcats were busy painting a mural on the back wall of the game room. The design was very contemporary, with large colorful shapes sprawling across the wide wall. The choice of colors definitely brightened the room and made the area feel like a really fun place.

"Looking good!" Taylor called over to Martha. She walked closer to the mural to examine the work. "That is a really cool design, and I love the colors."

Martha looked up as she dipped her brush into a can of fresh paint. "Thanks!" she exclaimed, blushing. "It's really coming out nicely, huh? The kids had the idea for this design." She took a step back to examine the wall. "We're almost done," Martha told Taylor. "Don't worry. We're going to head over to the theater after we're finished. I have a feeling that all these paints and brushes will come in handy for whatever set is needed for the show."

"Good thinking," Taylor responded. As she walked back to the study room, she saw Sue walk in. The quiet, dark-haired girl quickly went over to an empty table and took out a book and started reading. Taylor watched her for a minute, and then decided to go and sit next to her.

"Hey, Sue," Taylor said cheerfully. "I thought that you could help me with something. Would you mind if I sat down here?"

Sue looked up at Taylor with her large brown eyes. She looked really nervous.

Taylor continued. "I was thinking that maybe

you'd like to help me with some trivia questions for a quiz bowl we're planning at school next week," she explained. She pulled out the chair next to her and quickly sat down before Sue could object. She reached into her backpack for a stack of note cards. "Can I ask you some questions to see if they're any good?"

Sue nodded her head. "Great," Taylor said. "Here's the first one. What is the capital of Minnesota?"

"St. Paul," Sue answered.

Taylor looked at another note card. "What's the capital of Spain?"

"Madrid," Sue responded without missing a beat.

Taylor raised her eyebrows. Sue was really smart! Taylor decided to give her a harder question. She flipped through a few cards. "What's the capital of Switzerland?" she asked.

A smile started to spread across Sue's face. "That's easy," she quipped. "Bern."

Taylor was ecstatic. This had been the moment

that she had been waiting for—a real smile on Sue's face! Taylor couldn't help but smile back at her. Finally, she had made a connection! "You're really good at trivia," Taylor said.

Sue blushed and looked down at her hands. "I guess," Sue replied softly. "Do you like trivia, too?"

Taylor's eyes popped open. "Do I like trivia?" she repeated. "I do!" she cried. She leaned in closer to Sue. "When I was your age, I started to realize that learning trivia was really fun and I never stopped studying. I have a ton of books that I could lend you." She put her arm around Sue's shoulders. "Hey, maybe one day you'll be head of the East High Scholastic Decathlon team, too!"

"Just like you?" Sue asked, her eyes shining brightly.

Taylor smiled. She wasn't even sure how Sue had known that she was part of the Scholastic Decathlon team, but she was glad that they had found something to bond over. "Yes," Taylor replied. "Just like me." Taylor was so relieved. She couldn't wait to share the news with Gabriella later!

Sharpay walked into the theater at the community center feeling confident. After her talk with Ms. Darbus, she had decided to really give directing a chance. Today's rehearsal would be different. She was ready. She could play this role. But Sharpay wasn't ready for what she found onstage. She dropped her bag and her mouth gaped open when she switched on the lights of the theater.

"Surprise!" Ryan called out. He spread his hands in front of his face in his trademark jazz-hands style. Behind Ryan stood a stage full of Wildcats. They were all standing there smiling at Sharpay.

"What is going on?" she asked, confused.

"We're here to help," Kelsi said, stepping forward. "If you'd like help," she added.

Sharpay was stunned. While she didn't want

to confess that she needed help, she had to admit that having everyone involved would make the production much better. She turned her back to gather her thoughts, quickly reviewed all that Ms. Darbus had said, and then faced the crowd on the stage.

"The positions of stage manager, choreographer, and musical director are all open," Sharpay reported, without losing her cool. "Is anyone interested in those positions?"

"Well, it just so happens that I have some new music that would be perfect for the show," Kelsi said. She sat down at the piano and started to play. The song had a funky rhythm, and immediately a bunch of people started to move to the music. Sharpay walked over to the piano and stood behind Kelsi.

"Did you just write that?" Sharpay asked, peering over Kelsi's shoulder. The melody was really catchy and fun.

"No," Kelsi told her as she continued to play. "James Connelly did. He is one of the kids Ryan and I have been working with in our songwriting sessions."

"Oh," Sharpay murmured. She listened to the rest of the song, tapping her foot. "This would be great. The music has a really good rhythm." She looked over at Ryan. "Don't you think?"

Ryan nodded his head and smiled at his sister. "I think I can choreograph something to that," he said. He looked over at Martha. "But I'd love some help. What do you say?"

Martha took a moment to consider Ryan's request. She had never really thought of herself as a choreographer, but she did love to dance. A smile started to form on her face and then quickly turned into a wide grin. "Sure, count me in!" she exclaimed. "I'd love to help out!" She did a few quick hip-hop moves and everyone cheered.

Dancing over to her, Ryan nodded his head. "This is an awesome song! We're going to rock this show out!"

The group formed a circle around Ryan and Martha as they started to dance. Gabriella grabbed Troy's hand and pulled him into the circle. Their enthusiasm was contagious, and soon they were all dancing onstage. Taylor and Chad, Sharpay and Zeke—everyone was having a blast!

Relieved, Sharpay enjoyed the scene in front of her. She caught Ryan's eye across the stage and smiled at him.

Just then Sharpay spotted Hannah, Carly, Rosie, and the other kids who had signed up to be in the show walking into the auditorium, ready for rehearsal.

"Wow!" Hannah said to her sister Carly. "Are all these people going to help with our show?" She gasped when she saw who was on the stage. "The whole cast of *Twinkle Towne* is here!"

Gabriella overheard the little girl's comment and smiled. "We definitely are!" she exclaimed. She motioned for Hannah to join the group onstage.

Hannah and the others climbed the steps to

the stage and gathered around the Wildcats.

"Is your name Gabriella?" Hannah asked shyly. "You were the star of *Twinkle Towne*, weren't you? You were amazing!"

Gabriella laughed. "Thank you so much," she said, blushing a deep red. "And now it's your turn to shine onstage."

Sharpay, who had been listening in on Gabriella's conversation, walked over to Ryan. "This show needed your touch," she told him gratefully.

Ryan looked at her and smiled. "You can do this, Sharpay," he said. "But it takes teamwork. It's a really big job."

Sharpay nodded her head. She had definitely realized that. But she was still the director! Now she really had to step up her game. With everyone involved, this show could really be something special. "A good director knows good help," Sharpay said crisply. "And I'm really glad that help showed up here today."

Ryan grinned. He knew that was hard for Sharpay to admit.

"This is going to be an amazing show!" Ryan cheered.

Kelsi began to play a song from *Twinkle Towne,* and everyone joined in, singing and dancing.

Sharpay watched Carly, Hannah, Rosie, Max, and the other kids dancing around the stage. They were actually all pretty good dancers. And with Ryan's choreography, they could be even better. This show is going to turn out fabulously, Sharpay thought. "Oh, we are definitely going to rock this show!" she exclaimed, grinning. "I'll make sure of it!"

CHAPTER NINE

Taylor looked over the display of senior notes that she had set up on a table by the front entrance of school. Carefully, she arranged the stacks of red-and-white cards into neat piles on a red tablecloth. She adjusted the Wildcats banner hanging from the front of the table, and then stood back to admire her work. She wanted every senior walking into school that morning to pass by—and buy a note!

"Sorry I'm late!" Martha called, popping her

head through one of the doors in the front entrance. "I had a hard time getting all these here." With a gentle tug, she pulled a dozen red and white balloons through the doorway.

"Perfect!" Taylor exclaimed, walking over to help Martha. The balloons definitely added some pizazz to the display. The girls quickly tied the balloons to the legs of the table. "This looks really festive! Good for business, don't you think?"

Martha surveyed the table. "Definitely," she said.

Just then, Wylie Wildcat came bounding down the hallway. He slid dramatically over to the display table just as the first few students walked into school.

"Ryan!" Taylor cheered. "I'm so glad you showed! I think that it'll really help sales to have you here." Then she giggled. "I mean, to have *Wylie* here."

Ryan saluted with his paw and did a funky dance that attracted lots of attention from the

East High students walking by. There were whoops and cheers as the Wildcat mascot showed off his awesome moves.

As Taylor watched him dance, she knew that asking him to perform at the senior note sale was a stroke of genius. Already she could see that having Wylie there added lots of excitement to the morning.

Ryan finished his energetic routine and pointed both paws to the table, where Taylor and Martha were ready to take the students' orders.

"Good morning!" Taylor greeted the East High students now standing around the table. "Buy a senior note to send to a friend!" she called out. "Let someone know how you feel, and raise money for this year's senior project at the Wellington Community Center."

"You can bring the sealed notes back later," Martha added. "Take your time to write the perfect letter."

"This looks great!" Gabriella exclaimed as she and Troy walked over to the table.

"I'll take one," Troy said. He winked at Gabriella as he pulled out his wallet. "I think I've got a few things to say to a certain Wildcat."

Gabriella tossed her head back, trying to be coy. "Me, too," she said, reaching out for a note card. "There's one Wildcat in particular who's going to get a special note from me."

"Oh, so sweet," Martha cooed as she sold them both note cards. "Get these back to us by Friday and we'll deliver them during homeroom next week."

Wylie started to jump up and down and wave his arms. Taylor laughed and leaned closer to Martha.

"Um, Mr. Wildcat over there has volunteered to do the delivering," she said, pointing to the oversized cat.

They all laughed as more and more seniors came up to the table. Taylor was very pleased.

"We can sell more notes during lunch," she told Martha. "I have a feeling this is going to be a record sale for the notes."

"Oh, senior notes!" Kelsi exclaimed when she saw the table. "This really makes me feel like a senior. Getting one of these is special."

Taylor grinned. "I know," she said. "It's a note to treasure forever." She got a wistful look on her face. "I can't wait to see what Chad writes to me!"

The two friends giggled, failing to notice that Chad was standing right behind them. He quickly ducked behind two other students and made his way down the hallway dribbling a basketball. Weaving in and out of the crowd, he safely moved through the hall to homeroom without being spotted. He slipped into Ms. Darbus's room and into his seat. When he sat down, he finally exhaled deeply.

Oh, no, thought Chad. If Taylor is thinking all that, the pressure is on! He had no clue what to write in a senior note. And if Taylor was expecting something special, he was in trouble. *Big* trouble.

Before he had a chance to think more about his dilemma, the bell rang and everyone filed into the room. Ms. Darbus walked to the front of the class, beaming.

"There's a special announcement today," she sang out. "Please, everyone, take your seats. Principal Matsui will be addressing the school very shortly."

The class sat down and waited for the announcements to begin.

"Good morning, students!" Principal Matsui's voice finally boomed through the intercom system. "Before the regular announcements this morning, I would like to tell you all that the faculty has elected Martha Cox as the chair for the Senior Breakfast, which takes place next week. We applaud all of Martha's hard work this year on several committees and on the cheerleading squad, as well as her fine academic achievements. Please join me in congratulating Martha!"

Ms. Darbus's homeroom erupted in applause. Martha blushed as she stood up at her seat and took a bow. She was totally surprised!

"Thanks, everyone," Martha finally managed to say. "I'm really honored. And I promise to make our Senior Breakfast this year a fun time. We'll definitely have some good music, that's for sure."

"And food!" Zeke yelled out from the back of the classroom. He caught Martha's eye. "If you need help in the kitchen, let me know," he said cheerfully.

"Yeah," Jason added. "Let me know if you need help with anything." He smiled at Martha, wanting to make a good impression.

Martha nodded her head. "You're on!" she exclaimed.

"Now, let's remember"—Ms. Darbus directed them—"this breakfast is also for the faculty to attend, so keep that in mind."

"Of course," Martha said, sitting back down in her seat. "Don't worry, Ms. Darbus. I won't let you down."

"I'm sure you won't," Ms. Darbus replied. "We're all looking forward to the event."

Popping up out of her seat, Martha added, "And don't forget that we're having a set-painting party today at the community center. Please come by after you've finished volunteering to help out if you can."

"Yes," Sharpay added, perking up. "Martha and I discussed the themes, and we've decided on a suitable backdrop."

Ms. Darbus looked over at Sharpay and nodded her head. She was glad that Sharpay had chosen to work with her classmates on the musical.

Gabriella couldn't wait to get to the center. Now that she had gotten Henry into the water, she was hoping he would be ready to learn how to swim. She had done a little extra research the previous night and had found some new games that she hoped would get Henry into the pool again. Only a few more hours to go, she thought, as she looked up at the clock on the wall. This senior project was turning out to be more special to her than she would have thought.

Troy leaned against the wall, waiting for Gabriella. He checked his watch. She was supposed to be out of the locker room by now. All of their friends were waiting for them at the theater for the set-painting party. It wasn't like Gabriella to be late. He checked his cell phone. No messages.

"Hey," Gabriella called softly, tapping Troy on the shoulder.

Troy slid his phone back into his pocket and smiled. "How'd Henry do today?" he asked. He knew how much she was hoping that today would be the day where Henry would be ready to learn how to swim.

"We didn't have a great day today," she said sadly. "Henry didn't want to put his head in the water. We played a game, and he got water on his face, and he freaked out. He jumped out of the pool, and then he wouldn't get back in!"

Trying not to get too emotional, Gabriella went on to explain to Troy what had happened at the lesson. Mr. Hall had tried to ease her mind, but she had felt awful. Henry had trusted her. Now she felt that she had blown her chances with him.

"Poor Henry," Troy said. He shook his head. "There's always tomorrow's class," he said brightly, trying to boost her spirits.

Gabriella looked down at her feet. "If Henry even comes back tomorrow," she mumbled. "And here I was thinking that we had made so much progress. Now he's traumatized!"

"Maybe not," Troy offered. "Why not see what tomorrow brings? Henry might surprise you." He gave Gabriella a gentle push and then pulled at her hand. "Come on, we have a set-painting party to go to down the hall,"

As Gabriella and Troy walked to the auditorium, Troy spotted Rosie walking toward them. She was becoming one of his favorites on the team. Her energy and spirit were a close match for her natural athletic ability. She was just elected captain of the team, too!

"Hey, Troy!" Rosie called.

Gabriella smiled when she saw how Rosie's whole face lit up when she saw him. It was nice to see Troy helping out younger kids. He was so good at coaching basketball, she mused, just like his dad.

"Hi, Rosie," Troy said. "Great playing today. You looked like a real pro out there. And now you're the team captain!" He put out his hand to give her a high five. "How does that feel?"

"Great," Rosie replied happily. Her smile grew wider. "We have a chance to win against Southside, don't you think?"

"You bet!" Troy cheered. "Teamwork! You all have to remember that. Pacing the ball is key. That's how games are won."

As they stood in the hall, Gabriella realized that she had seen Rosie before—but not on the court. She was one of the girls who had danced onstage with Sharpay the day before. "You're in the show, too, right?" Gabriella asked.

Rosie quickly looked down at the ground as they walked toward the auditorium. "Well, I was," she said softly. "But I'm not sure I'm going to be in the show anymore."

"Why?" Gabriella asked. She remembered Rosie as one of the best dancers up on the stage that day. "You can really dance!"

"Thanks," Rosie said. She looked up at Gabriella. "I saw you two at East High when you were in a play. My older brother goes there. You guys were really good!"

Troy blushed. He was used to people commenting on his basketball playing, but it was still new to him to hear all the rave reviews of his stage performances.

Rosie turned to Troy. "How did you get into singing?" she asked.

Troy laughed. He pointed to Gabriella. "It's all her fault," he teased.

"*My* fault?" Gabriella argued, laughing. "I don't know about that. I think you had the bug in you all along." She smiled at Rosie. "But I guess that I did have a little to do with pushing him to try out for *Twinkle Towne* last year."

Troy gently squeezed Gabriella's hand, and they shared a smile.

Rosie looked over at them and sighed. Troy made it look so easy to be a basketball player *and* an actor. But she wasn't so sure that she could do that.

"How come you asked how I got into singing?" Troy said as they arrived at the auditorium doors.

"Oh, I don't know," Rosie said nervously. "I gotta go," she called over her shoulder as she took off down the hall.

"Wait," Troy called after her. "Aren't you going to come to rehearsal today?"

Rosie stopped and turned around. "Um, I can't go today," she said. She turned quickly and raced off.

Troy watched Rosie disappear and then looked over at Gabriella. "What do you think that was all about?"

"Not sure," Gabriella said. "Maybe you should talk to her?"

"Yeah," Troy replied. "I think I definitely should."

"Hey, painters!" Martha called as she came up behind them. "Glad that you came! Welcome to the set-painting party!" She pulled some brushes from her pocket. "Here—grab one of these and head to the stage. There's lots to paint." She pointed straight ahead to the stage.

There were already a few Wildcats at center stage painting two large murals. The stereo was blaring, and everyone looked as if they were having a good time.

"You see, Gabriella," Troy said with a sly grin, "there's nothing that we can't do with some teamwork!"

"You're absolutely right, captain," Gabriella said, tapping her paintbrush softly on Troy's head. "Let's go join the painting team. And make this show happen!"

They both walked up to the stage to join their friends. If Gabriella couldn't help Henry today, at least she could help out with the sets and the show. The Wildcats were on call to help the center, and she wanted to be a part of that show for sure!

CHAPTER TEN

The next day, Chad spotted Gabriella walking through the East High cafeteria. When he finally caught up to her, she vanished in a crowd of students. Oh, boy, he thought. Of course, it has to be pizza day, when the lines are mega long! How was he going to get to talk to her now?

Chad pushed his way through the crowded line, searching for her. He saw her re-emerge in front of the salad bar and raced over to her. The lunch crowd was aggressive, so Chad had to use his best on-court moves to make it through the long line of Wildcats. He tried to be nonchalant and play it cool. He ducked around the last few people in his way, catching up to Gabriella just as she was paying for her lunch.

"Hey, Gabriella!" Chad called, a little out of breath.

"Hi, Chad," she replied. She eyed his empty hands. "You're waiting in line and you don't have a tray?"

"Oh, I was just . . ." Chad looked around and grabbed an apple from the bowl by the register. "I was just coming back for a snack," he said, trying to keep his composure. He didn't want Gabriella to know how he'd been waiting for her to come to the cafeteria so that he could have a few minutes alone with her before Taylor arrived. He knew that Taylor had a senior project meeting with Ms. Darbus for a few minutes at the beginning of the period, so he had to act fast. If he wanted time alone with Gabriella, now was his only shot.

"What's going on?" Gabriella asked, carefully eyeing Chad. She quickly walked over to a table to sit down, with Chad trailing closely behind her.

"So," Chad began. He looked down at the apple in his hand, twisting the stem around and around until it came off. "I was hoping for a little help."

Placing her lunch tray on the table, Gabriella looked up at Chad. "Of course," she said. She sat down and pulled out the chair next to her for Chad to sit down.. "What is it?"

Chad slid down into the chair. "Well, first you have to promise not to say a word to Taylor." Not sure what Chad was going to say next, Gabriella looked a bit hesitant. "It's nothing bad," he said quickly. He held up his hand like a surrendering warrior. "Honest."

Gabriella nodded her head. "All right," she said. "Spill it."

"The senior notes," Chad whispered. He glanced over his shoulder to make sure no one was listening to their conversation. "They are such a big deal to Taylor, and I just . . ." He stopped as he searched for the right words. He looked up at Gabriella's kind eyes and he continued on. "I just don't know what she expects me to say to her in the note! I'm not really the best writer."

Smiling, Gabriella shook her head. "Oh, Chad," she told him. She reached out and put her hand on his arm. "Taylor just wants you to write something from your heart. Something real."

Chad's curls flopped around as he threw his head back. "But I don't think like that!" he cried. "Man, I'm in trouble. What am I going to say? I mean what would Taylor want me to say?" He took a bite of the apple in his hand, taking a minute to pull his thoughts together. He looked down at the floor as he continued. "These senior notes are just ridiculous. Who really cares about that kind of stuff anyway?"

As Chad said those words, he lifted his head

up. He watched Gabriella's face go pale. She couldn't say a thing, but just pointed her finger over his shoulder. Chad slowly turned in his seat and followed where her finger was directing him. As he did, his breath got caught in his chest. He felt as if he had been socked in the stomach. Standing right behind him was—Taylor!

From the look on Taylor's face, she had definitely overheard what he had just said. And probably just the last part! Oh, no! Chad sprang up out of his chair. He knew this all looked *and* sounded bad! How would he be able to explain this one?

"Is that so?" Taylor snapped, glaring at Chad. Her hands were firmly planted on her hips, and she narrowed her eyes as she spoke. "You don't see why *anyone* would want a senior note? Well, perhaps you don't get it. But I do! You know what? I don't want a senior note from you. Or *anything* to do with you!" She turned on her heel and stomped away.

"I was trying to warn you," Gabriella said to Chad. "But she just snuck up so fast!" She reached out to put her hand on his. "I'll talk to her," she said reassuringly. "She's under a lot of pressure, you know. All these senior activities and meetings. There's a lot going on here. There's just so much to do!"

"Oh, I know," Chad said. "And now I'm under pressure, too. If I can't win Taylor back with a stellar senior note, my chances of going to the prom with her are nil, not to mention making my life here at East High somewhat unbearable for the next couple of weeks!" He looked over at the kitchen and saw Taylor huffing and puffing as she reached for her lunch. She was grabbing at items and throwing them on her tray. When she was this mad, there was nothing anyone could do until she cooled off.

"I'm going to let her calm down," Chad told Gabriella. He stood up and pushed his chair into the table. "And then I'm going to surprise her and write her the best note she could ever get!" He looked back at Gabriella, his eyes full of hope. "It will all work out, right?" he asked her.

"I'm sure that everything will work out just fine," she said, trying to sound positive. She could see that Chad felt awful about Taylor's reaction. "Let me know if I can help you in any way."

Chad shot her a grateful look. "I'll let you know." He turned to leave and then turned around again. "Thanks, Gabriella. I appreciate your support."

"You got it," she replied. "And for what it's worth, I think that you'll do a great job with Taylor's note. Don't worry."

"Thanks," he said. Only he didn't really believe that he could possibly write anything that would fix the mess that he had just gotten himself into. He had just committed a foul that no referee would let him get away with. He was going to have to earn his way back into the game. And *fast*.

By the time Taylor returned to the table, Chad

was gone. Gabriella moved her tray over and made room for her friend.

"It wasn't what you thought," Gabriella said as soon as Taylor sat down. Even though Gabriella had promised Chad that she wouldn't divulge his secret about not knowing what to write for a senior note, she wanted Taylor to realize that she should at least have some sympathy for him.

But that didn't seem to be happening any time too soon.

"Haven't I been to every one of his games?" Taylor asked snippily. She ripped off the plastic wrap on her sandwich and crumpled it into a tiny ball. Then she shot the plastic-wrap ball through the air for a perfect two-pointer in the nearest trash can. "I've been to *more* than my share of basketball games this year."

"Yes, you have," Gabriella remarked. "And that was a very nice shot, I might add." She winked at Taylor. "Oh, cut him some slack, Taylor," she urged her friend.

Taking a bite of her sandwich, Taylor shook her head. "No way. Absolutely not. These senior notes *are* a big deal to me. If he can't understand that, well, then we have nothing to say to each other."

Gabriella looked down at her tray. She knew that wasn't the case at all. Chad *did* know how much the notes meant to Taylor, he just didn't know what to write to her! Gabriella hoped he'd figure something out. She knew that even though Taylor was mad, she really cared about Chad. Gabriella hated it when her friends were unhappy or didn't get along.

"Hey, there!" Martha called, coming up to their table. She sat down across from Gabriella and Taylor. "I'm so excited about the Senior Breakfast! I've already come up with some ideas. It's going to be so much fun."

"Me, too," Gabriella said. "What are you planning?"

"Well," Martha began, "I was thinking that we should definitely use our school colors as part of the breakfast theme. Red and white are cool colors, so we should use them for our decorations."

Even though Taylor was still mad at Chad, she couldn't help but get involved with the conversation. "We don't have a ton of money for the breakfast," she told Martha. "We have to stay within the budget. So keep that in mind when you are planning."

Gabriella kicked Taylor's leg under the table. She wanted her to snap out of the bad mood her fight with Chad had left her in and focus on what Martha was saying.

"Ouch!" cried Taylor, reaching down to rub her leg. She looked over at Gabriella. Then she realized that Martha was still sitting at their table, anxiously awaiting her response. "Well, red and white seem like a good place to start," she said, trying to sound enthusiastic.

Martha nodded. "Don't worry, Ms. Darbus gave me all the rules," she replied. "But I was thinking that if we were creative, we could really make the budget stretch. You know, and make the breakfast something different and a little unique."

Troy, Zeke, and Jason appeared at the end of their table, each holding a lunch tray. The girls quickly made room for the boys.

"What's cooking?" Zeke asked. He slid his tray down across from Gabriella.

"We're talking about the Senior Breakfast," Martha told them. "I was thinking that we definitely have to decorate the entire room in red and white since they're our school colors."

"Oh, and I know just the perfect dessert to serve after breakfast!" Zeke piped up. All eyes turned to focus on him. "My famous Wildcats cake! And maybe at breakfast we could have some berry scones—you know, to play off our school colors."

Troy slapped Zeke on the back. "See, that's why it's so amazing to have a chef on hand!" he exclaimed. "You rock!"

Martha was jotting down notes in her

notebook. "Hold on," she said, still writing. Her pen was flying across the page at lightning speed. "I want to make sure I have all those ideas." She looked up and grinned at Zeke. "Thanks, Chef Zeke!"

"You know what else would be cool?" Jason said. "If we played music at our breakfast, too. Maybe some of the kids from the school band can come and perform."

"Great idea!" Martha exclaimed, smiling. "That would be really fun!"

"Me, too," Gabriella added.

"It sounds like this will be the perfect Senior Breakfast," Taylor said. "Nice job."

Martha grinned. "Thanks, everyone!" she cried as she gathered up her things. "This is going to be one rockin' Senior Breakfast!"

Gabriella noticed the strained smile on Taylor's face. She assumed that Taylor was still thinking about what she had overheard Chad saying about the senior notes. She hoped that Taylor would forgive Chad . . . and that Chad would get his act together and write her an awesome note. She smiled to herself and finished up her lunch. She had faith in Chad—she knew that he'd come through. Now if she could just believe that she could come through for Henry and help him out. She hoped today's swimming lesson would go much better than the last one. Gabriella knew that she had to work extra hard this afternoon to get Henry back in the water. But she was going to give it her best shot. Henry had to get in the water—he just had to!

CHAPTER ELEVEN

The familiar smell of chlorine greeted Gabriella as she pulled open the door between the locker room and the pool. The scent took her back to her earliest memories of swimming laps with her mom Saturday mornings at their community pool. Unlike Henry, Gabriella was never afraid of the water. In fact, her mom used to call her a fish. Gabriella never wanted to get out of the pool.

Taking a deep breath, Gabriella peered

around the pool, hoping that Henry was there, but she didn't see him anywhere. After swimming class the day before, she hadn't felt sure that Henry would come back to the center. She feared that he'd want to stay far away from the pool. The splashing from the game had really set him back.

"Hi, Gabriella!" Mr. Hall called from the diving area. He was holding a clipboard in one hand and waving with the other. "Good to see you!"

Joining Mr. Hall, Gabriella walked with him over to the shallow end of the pool. She looked over his shoulder to get a glimpse of his clipboard. "Any chance you've heard from Henry?" she asked.

"Not yet," he said. "But a few of the kids aren't here yet." He pointed to his attendance sheet. "Let's hope for the best." He lifted his whistle to his mouth and blew a long note. The whistle got everyone's attention, and all the kids standing around the pool went to sit along the edge at the shallow end.

"I know that you've been working with Henry," Mr. Hall said quietly. "Let's hope that he comes today so we can get him back into the water. He was doing so well. You should be very proud of your work."

I don't feel proud at all, Gabriella thought. If she hadn't made Henry play that game, he wouldn't have gotten splashed. And maybe he would be at the pool today. She looked down.

Mr. Hall looked at her sympathetically. "It's not your fault that he got splashed yesterday," he told her, seeming to read her mind. "In a way it was good for him. He got splashed, and he was actually okay. You'll see," he said with a wink. "I bet Henry comes back today. Let's see what happens." He looked Gabriella in the eyes. "But no special treatment. I'd like him to get back in the pool of his own free will."

Trying not to feel disappointed, Gabriella moved along with the kids to the pool. She knew that Mr. Hall was probably right, but she couldn't help but feel that she had let Henry down. Would he get back in the pool? Looking at the faces of the other kids in the class, Gabriella realized that there were more kids there to teach. She couldn't mope around worrying about Henry. She jumped into the water as Mr. Hall began the lesson of the day.

As she turned to drag the stack of kickboards toward the water, Gabriella saw Henry sitting on the edge of the bottom bleacher at the far end of the pool, wearing his swimsuit and a sweatshirt. Her eyes widened in surprise, and she wanted to run over to him and let him know how happy she was that he was there. But she knew that any sudden move would send Henry scurrying back into the locker room. She had to play it cool and let Henry come to the pool on his own. Mr. Hall was right. She knew this was a gamble, but Henry had to do it by himself. She got the kickboards from the side of the pool and handed them out to the class. As she passed Mr. Hall, she motioned toward where Henry was sitting.

He nodded his head and went on teaching the class.

Ten minutes later, Henry moved closer to the shallow end, where the class was bopping around in the water. He still had his sweatshirt on, but he had made an effort to move closer. Gabriella still didn't look up and tried not to catch his gaze. She wanted to wait for him to come to the edge of the pool. Hoping that he'd make it there before the end of class, she tried to focus on the other kids.

Finally, with about ten minutes left in the hour-long class, Henry slung his feet into the pool and unzipped his sweatshirt. He swished his feet back and forth in the water, watching the other kids.

"Henry," Mr. Hall said, slowly approaching him. "Would you like to have a turn with the kickboard?" He handed him a board, and then turned his attention to the others in the class.

From across the pool, Gabriella watched as

Henry took off his sweatshirt and slid into the water. He gripped the edge of the board and joined the rest of the class as they all lined up against the wall. Henry was not only in the water, he was participating with the whole class! Gabriella couldn't believe it. She couldn't help but beam as she watched Henry kick his way across the length of the pool. He was keeping his head down and didn't seem bothered by all the splashing from the kicking around him.

When everyone reached the other side, they all raised their kickboards in the air and let out a roaring cheer.

Henry's smile lifted Gabriella's spirits. She felt good knowing that Henry had tackled his fear of the water. And he had done it all by himself. She waded over to him and held out her hand to give him a high five.

"Nice lap, Henry," she told him. "You did great!"

Henry blushed. "Thanks," he said. "I remembered what you said about keeping my head down and kicking my feet."

Gabriella laughed. "Good! See, I told you that you could do it! Just like Rufus does at the lake, right?"

Nodding his head up and down, Henry agreed. "But I think that I'm actually faster than Rufus," he said proudly.

Gabriella reached out and ruffled Henry's wet hair. "I believe that, Henry," she told him. "You're a fast swimmer."

Mr. Hall looked over and grinned. He gave Gabriella and Henry both a thumbs up.

"Come on, Henry," Gabriella said. "I'll race you back to the other side of the pool." As she swam back with Henry kicking beside her, Gabriella realized that all the kids were joining in their race. She felt like a little kid again. It was the best feeling!

Troy was waiting for Gabriella right outside the locker-room door. When he saw Gabriella burst through the door, her hair still wet from the pool and her eyes shining, he knew that today's lesson had gone much better than yesterday's.

"Hi!" Gabriella exclaimed when she saw Troy. She couldn't wait to fill him in on the swimming lesson.

Troy grinned. "So Henry came back, huh?" he said, smiling. "Good for him!"

Gabriella grabbed Troy's arm. "It was amazing! He actually spent the whole class inching his way over to the pool. But then he got in, and he did a kickboard lap!"

Troy spun Gabriella around in a circle. "Hooray for Henry!" he cheered. "And hooray for his very patient and caring teacher."

Blushing, Gabriella shook her head. "It was all Henry. I'm so proud of him." As they walked down the hall, Gabriella turned to Troy. "How was the practice today? Is the team coming together?"

"Yup," Troy told her. "All those drills that my dad always makes us do really make a difference!" Then he stopped walking and faced

Gabriella. "I'm a little concerned about Rosie, though."

"Did you get a chance to talk to her?" she asked. "What happened today at practice?"

"Well, remember when she was asking me all those questions about being in the show?" he asked. "I heard from a few people that Rosie wasn't planning on showing up at rehearsal again today. When I asked her about it at practice, she just shrugged my questions off."

"That's strange," Gabriella commented. "She seemed so into the musical. And she is a really good dancer."

"I know," Troy sighed. "Would you mind swinging by the music room with me? I told Rosie that I'd see her there after practice. She was supposed to meet with Kelsi to go over a song. I made her promise to meet me there."

How could Gabriella turn down that invitation? "Sure," she said. "I'd be happy to go. I'd love to hear the songs for the musical. I bet the music is going to be great. Remember the song

Kelsi was playing, the one that James, the kid in her songwriting class, wrote?"

"James is on the basketball team, too!" Troy exclaimed. "We have a very talented team," he stated proudly.

In the music room, Kelsi was sitting at the piano, playing. She stopped when her friends walked in. "Hey, there!" she exclaimed.

Troy looked around the room. "Rosie's not here yet?" he asked.

"I'm here," Rosie said, walking in behind him.

Troy grinned. He was so happy that she had showed up.

Kelsi started playing the piano again. She nodded her head for the three of them to make their way over to her. "Come on over and start singing," she directed. "I think you'll like this one."

Rosie's hand flew to her mouth. "I can't just sing by myself!" she gasped.

Troy grabbed her hand. "We'll help you out. It's nice to start out singing together, right, Gabriella?" He held out his other hand to Gabriella.

Taking Troy's cue, Gabriella joined them at the piano. She glanced down at the song sheet that Kelsi handed her. "'Oh, when I hear the music, my heart starts beating,'" she sang.

"'It's the rhythm of the music that gets me going, going to where I need to be,'" Troy sang out. He pointed to Rosie, whose wide blue eyes were locked on Kelsi.

Kelsi played the music again, but Rosie remained quiet. "Come on, Rosie, you can do this," she said encouragingly. She played the first note again and sang softly, "'The music is the beat of my day and my heart.'" She repeated the chords again, looking right at her. "Try singing. You can do it."

This time, when Kelsi played the chords, Rosie sang out the words. Her clear, crisp voice caught them all by surprise. Her pitch was perfect and the melody seemed to soar when Rosie sang.

"Wow!" Troy exclaimed. "See, Rosie, you are really good at this!"

Rosie's face turned bright red. "Really?" she asked. "I've never actually sung in front of people—along with someone playing a piano!" She spun around happily. "This is a little different from singing by myself in my bedroom. I'm used to being center court—not center of attention!"

"Ah," Troy said, stepping closer to her. "Not really. Being at center court makes you feel like you're alive, right?"

Rosie nodded her head.

"Well, being center stage has that same power," Troy explained. "When I sing a song, it feels amazing!"

Gabriella and Kelsi shared a smile. Watching Troy help Rosie break out of her shell to sing was awesome.

"I used to hate singing in front of people," Gabriella added. "But Troy is right, when you sing—especially with a voice as beautiful as yours—it's the best feeling. Try the song again from the top."

"Close your eyes and pretend that no one else is here," Kelsi advised. "Just listen to the music, and don't think about anything else."

As Rosie sang the song James had written, Gabriella, Troy, and Kelsi all nodded and smiled. Rosie was perfect!

"I think we just got our lead!" Kelsi exclaimed happily.

Rosie looked startled. "Wait, Hannah is the lead! I'm just a basketball player!"

Troy started to laugh. "Oh, no," he moaned, hitting his hand on his forehead. "Not this again!"

Gabriella and Kelsi started to laugh.

"What do you mean?" Rosie asked, looking confused.

"Just because you like to play basketball doesn't mean that you can't star in the musical!" Troy exclaimed.

"I guess," Rosie said, still a bit unsure. "But

how am I going to tell Hannah? She'll be so disappointed!"

Kelsi put up her hand. "Don't worry about Hannah," she said. "She'll have a big part, too. But this song is all yours, Rosie. You deserve to have a solo."

"And you need to prove to yourself that you can be at center court *and* at center stage," Troy said with a wink. "I know you can do it."

Troy squeezed Gabriella's hand. If it hadn't had been for Gabriella, he never would have known what he was capable of doing. Now he had a chance to help someone else try to reach for their best. And that felt pretty great!

CHAPTER TWELVE

After Kelsi had finished playing through the song a few times, she put her hands in her lap and grinned up at Rosie. The young girl had nailed the song! She winked at Troy and Gabriella. They were smiling, too. Rosie's voice lent the perfect tone to the music, making the song absolutely perfect. With Ryan and Martha's choreography, the act was sure to be a show-stopper.

"Bravo!" Kelsi cheered. Kelsi watched as

Rosie blushed again and looked down at her sneakers.

"Thanks," she said shyly.

Kelsi stood up and gathered the music from the piano, then reached under the piano bench to put the music in her bag. "It was really great," she said honestly. "Believe me, I wouldn't say anything if it weren't true."

Troy and Gabriella echoed Kelsi's compliments. But now, when she heard their bravos, Rosie's eyes welled up with tears.

"What's wrong?" Gabriella asked, reaching out to her. She wasn't sure what had happened to make Rosie cry. Weren't they all just telling her how great she was?

"Hey, are you okay?" Troy asked, moving closer to Rosie. "What's going on?" He looked over at Gabriella and Kelsi, but they seemed just as surprised at Rosie's reaction. There was a long, awkward silence as they all listened to Rosie sniffle and sob.

Finally, Rosie looked up at the East High

seniors staring at her. She shook her head and took the tissue that Gabriella held out to her. "It's nothing," she mumbled as she wiped her nose. She turned to grab her book bag and started to head out of the room.

"*Nothing* doesn't make you burst into tears," Troy called as he chased after her. "Come on, talk to us." He put his hand gently on her shoulder, and steered her back over to the piano. "Talk to me," he said softly. "I'd like to help."

Taking a deep breath, Rosie slowly exhaled. Her wispy bangs fluttered up and down on her forehead. She hadn't told anyone how she was feeling about all this. And she definitely hadn't meant to burst into tears. She was so embarrassed. But looking up, she saw Troy smile at her. His blue eyes were focused on her, and she immediately felt that she could trust him.

"It's just that I haven't told my parents that I am going to be singing in the show, and I don't think they are going to be too happy," she blurted out while she stared down at her feet.

When she raised her eyes, she saw all three seniors smiling at her.

They totally don't get what I'm saying, Rosie thought. I never should have said anything! And to make matters worse, they are laughing at me!

"Oh, forget it," she said, rushing for the door again. "I shouldn't have opened my mouth. You wouldn't understand."

"Are you kidding?" Troy exclaimed. "I totally understand where you are coming from!" He started to laugh again. "We all know exactly what you mean. *That's* why we're laughing."

Rosie turned around and saw Troy beckoning her back to the piano.

As he waited for Rosie, Troy thought back on how nervous he had been about telling his parents how much he loved theater. He definitely understood why Rosie was feeling so overwhelmed. Telling his dad about being in *Twinkle Towne* was one of the hardest conversations that he had ever had with him. And his dad's reaction hadn't been the best. But he had come around once he realized how much the role meant to Troy, and what being part of the cast meant to him. When Troy's dad came and saw his son perform, he totally changed his tune. If Troy hadn't been honest with his dad, he wouldn't have had that opportunity to get closer to him.

"You've got to be honest with your parents," Troy told Rosie. "If they don't know how much performing in the show means to you, then you aren't telling them the truth. You have to be honest with them. Trust me, things will be better if you do."

"And they need to hear you!" Kelsi added. "Your voice is amazing!"

Gabriella put her arm around Rosie. "When someone has a voice like yours," she said, "you need to share it with everyone. You have a special gift. Talk to your parents."

Rosie smiled at Gabriella. "I guess you're right," she replied. "But how am I supposed to tell them?"

"The best way is to just be straight with them," Troy said.

"Being honest is the best way," Gabriella agreed. "Plus, you don't have to give up playing basketball."

Kelsi laughed. "Thank goodness the show and the game aren't at the same time. I had to live through that experience once, and it was very stressful!"

Both Troy and Gabriella laughed along with Kelsi as they remembered the time when all their friends had worked together to enable them to get to the tryouts for *Twinkle Towne*. The show had been scheduled for the same time as the state championship basketball game and the Scholastic Decathlon tournament! If it hadn't been for their friends all working together, they never would have pulled it off.

"I have a feeling that everything is going to be just fine," Troy said, tugging on Rosie's ponytail.

Rosie giggled. "Thanks again," she said. She gestured toward the door. "I really have to get going now." As she reached the doorknob, she turned back toward Troy. "I'll see you at rehearsal in a few minutes!" she exclaimed, and slipped out into the hallway.

"I can't believe that was what was upsetting her," Troy said as he sat down in a folding chair near the piano. "I thought I was the only singing basketball star!"

Gabriella laughed. "Nope, those are a dime a dozen!" she joked. She grinned at Troy, knowing that he had really helped Rosie out. This experience was turning out to be more than just a mandatory senior project. The time at the Wellington Community Center was really special.

"I'll see you at rehearsal, right?" Kelsi asked Troy and Gabriella.

"We wouldn't miss it," Troy told her.

Gabriella looked over at Troy. "I told Taylor that I'd swing by the study room to get her," she said. "Come with me?"

Troy nodded and followed Gabriella out the

door. He was feeling a little anxious for Rosie. She was still just a kid, and she was already feeling so much pressure! He was glad that he had been able to give her some advice.

"Look," Gabriella said, pointing. "There's Taylor. And that girl next to her must be Sue!" The two girls were huddled together at a table in the back of the room.

As Gabriella and Troy got closer to the table, they overhead part of their conversation.

"The square root of nine?" Sue repeated. "Oh, come on. That is too easy. It's three."

Troy poked Gabriella. He leaned over and whispered in her ear "Is that Mini-Taylor?"

Gabriella giggled. "I think that she's in training to take over the Scholastic Decathlon team in another eight years!"

"Hi!" Taylor exclaimed when she saw her friends. She introduced Sue, but the little girl was so shy that she didn't even want to look up to say hello. Taylor closed up the books in front of her. "This was a great session, Sue. Keep this up, and you'll be a scholastic champion, too!"

Gabriella could see a smile spread across Sue's face. Taylor had made so much progress with her! Once again, Gabriella was proud of her friends and the way they had jumped in to help all the kids at the center.

When Sue left the room, Taylor grabbed Gabriella's arm. "How smart is she? I wasn't doing square roots until fifth grade, and just look at her! She's only in third grade and she's rocking it!"

"With a tutor like you," Troy commented, "I'm sure Sue is going to be a superstar student."

Taylor laughed. "Thanks," she said. "And now let's go check out the real show down the hall. Martha showed me the finished backdrop—the scenery looks beautiful!"

The three of them made their way to the theater. Inside, the rehearsal had already begun. They heard Kelsi playing the piano while a group of girls sang onstage.

Squinting, Troy followed the girl in the center.

"Is it just my eyes," he said, rubbing them, "or does that girl look like a young Sharpay?"

"You mean because of how she's pushing her way to the front and center of the stage?" Taylor asked. "I'd say that she's got all of Sharpay's moves down."

Gabriella looked toward the stage. Hannah is definitely Sharpay's mini-me version, she thought. Hannah was really good, but the way Ryan had choreographed the dance, she was not supposed to be in the center. The song-and-dance number was supposed to be a group act, not a dance solo.

"Hold it!" Ryan shouted. He was leading the rehearsal today, while Sharpay shopped for costumes for the cast.

Everyone stopped moving, and Kelsi lifted her hands off the piano keys.

"Sharpay told me it's best to stand *here*," Hannah snipped. She put her hands on her hips and tossed her head.

"I'm sure she did," Ryan muttered. "But did

she also tell you the importance of listening to the choreographer?"

"Um, no," Hannah said. She shifted her weight, but kept her hip popped out to the side. "Actually, she didn't say anything like that."

"That figures," Ryan huffed. "Well, I suggest that if you want to look good out there at center stage, then you start listening to me."

Hannah nodded and stepped back into her place.

Ryan and Martha got the rest of the group in sync and then cued Kelsi to begin the song from the top—again.

Gabriella watched from her seat, happy that the center's theater was getting some use and thrilled that so many East High students were helping out. Even Sharpay was working together with everyone else to make sure that the show was a success. Ms. Darbus was so right about the theater bringing people together.

"Let's take it from the top!" Ryan called.

Gabriella squeezed Troy's hand as the curtain

opened and Rosie stepped out on the stage. She gave a little wave to them and then focused on the music and her dance steps. Up onstage, Rosie looked comfortable and happy.

"She's awesome!" Troy exclaimed, beaming. "She's my star forward *and* the star singer!"

"Just like someone else I know," Gabriella said with a smile as she settled back down in her seat to watch the show.

CHAPTER THIRTEEN

"**W**e need more red ones!" Martha shouted from the top of a ladder. She was reaching up to the corner of a large banner to hang more balloons. She wanted the entrance of the cafeteria to be under a red-and-white balloon arch. There wasn't much time before the East High faculty and the entire senior class would enter the cafeteria for the Senior Breakfast. She was really feeling the pressure!

"Hold on!" Taylor called. She weaved around

the handful of seniors helping to set up the room. As she made her way to Jason, who was manning the helium tank, she repeated the order. "More red!" she instructed.

"Got it!" Jason replied as he pulled more red balloons from a bag. He quickly inflated the balloons, and then he handed them to Gabriella, who tied white ribbons around the ends before giving them to Taylor.

"Ah, teamwork!" Chad exclaimed as he dribbled his basketball into the cafeteria. He smiled as he surveyed all the work being done to transform the cafeteria into a red-and-white haven. "This place looks pretty cool! There's some serious Wildcat spirit here."

Taylor, who was still not speaking to Chad, just scowled at him. She quickly turned around and rushed over to Martha carrying a handful of red balloons, without saying a word to him.

"Hey, Chad!" Jason called as he watched Taylor storm off. "Is it chilly in here or what? I think you brought in some frosty, cold air!"

Chad bounced the ball a few times. As hard as he had tried to get Taylor to talk to him, she still seemed pretty angry about his comments on the senior notes. And he was having a lot of trouble writing his note to Taylor. The pressure was really getting to him! By now he had failed at several attempts to come up with the perfect senior note. He only had a couple more days until the notes would be delivered. If he was going to win Taylor back, he had to brush up on his prose—and fast!

Chad smacked Jason gently on the back and made his way over to Troy, who was unloading boxes from a large cart. "Are these Zeke's pastries?" he asked, peering into one of the boxes.

"Yup," Troy said, walking over. "And don't try to sneak one. I have strict instructions to keep these off limits until the breakfast begins."

"Hmmm," Chad said, closing the lid of the box. "He really outdid himself here, huh?"

Gabriella came over to them and smiled. "Hey there, Chad," she said happily. "Glad that you came to help." She handed him a stack of place cards. "Can you put these over there?" she asked, pointing to a long table at the front of the room. "That's where the faculty members are going to sit."

Chad looked over and saw Taylor watching him. He took the cards cheerfully. "I'm here to help!" he exclaimed, loudly enough so that Taylor would hear him.

"Perfect," Gabriella said. "I need to go get the teachers' plaques from my locker. I'll be right back."

"We'll be here!" Chad yelled loudly, hoping that Taylor heard him. "You know, just all being helpful Wildcats!"

Troy smiled as he watched his best friend. Poor Chad! He was trying so hard to make a good impression on Taylor. And she was still giving him the cold shoulder!

When Taylor turned around, Chad faced Troy. "I'm trying, you know? It's those senior notes! If I don't come up with a good letter, I'm doomed. Benched. *Over*."

"You'll come up with something," Troy said, trying to console him. "You always do." He lifted the last box of pastries and put them on the table. "Taylor just wants you to try."

"Hmmm," muttered Chad. He couldn't miss this shot with Taylor. This was like standing on the foul line to shoot in the final seconds of a game. He had to get the ball in the net. Nothing less would do.

"Oh, no!" Martha cried. She was looking up at the clock. "Has anyone seen the band? They were supposed to be here by eight." She glanced down at her watch. "I really want them to be playing when everyone walks in."

"We're here!" a voice called from the side door of the cafeteria. In walked East High's jazz band, decked out in their red jackets and white pants. They each carried their instruments and music stands in and began to set up in the corner of the room.

Martha beamed. Everything was coming together perfectly. She couldn't have been happier!

"The cafeteria really looks festive," Ryan told her as he walked in. In support of the themed breakfast, Ryan was sporting a red cap and jacket. He peered over at the food that Troy and Zeke were setting out on trays. "Zeke's pastries look delicious. And look at the awesome Wildcats cake!"

"Thanks!" Zeke exclaimed, overhearing the compliment. He watched the door for Sharpay to make her entrance. Sure enough, Sharpay soon swept into the room. She was wearing a short white leather jacket with a red skirt and tall white boots. Zeke sighed when he saw her. Sharpay had a way of melting his heart. She was a vision of Wildcat spirit!

"Greetings, Wildcats!" she called as she pranced around the room. "Where should I set up?" she asked Martha when she reached her on the other side of the room. "I brought my own microphone and sound equipment." She snapped her fingers, and two freshman boys appeared, struggling to carry a portable sound system. Before Martha had a chance to answer,

Sharpay surveyed the room and scoped out the best spot. "Just set it up over there," Sharpay directed the boys.

Taylor rolled her eyes. She wasn't thrilled with Martha's choice of Sharpay as master of ceremonies for the breakfast. She feared that the breakfast would quickly turn into a one-woman show starring Sharpay.

"Good morning, students!" Ms. Darbus sang out as she waltzed into the decorated cafeteria. "What festive decorations!" She whirled around and found Martha. "You did a wonderful job here, Martha. You should be very proud."

Martha smiled. Then she waved around at all her friends in the room. "I couldn't have done this without all their help."

"I'm glad to see you're all working together," Ms. Darbus said as she walked past the pastries. "Oh, Zeke, these look remarkable. And look at that beautiful cake! It looks delicious!"

"Hopefully, you'll think it tastes that way, too," Zeke said with a grin.

"I'm confident that they will," Principal Matsui said as he walked over to the table. "This looks absolutely wonderful," he commented, looking around at the platters of fruit salad, bagels, and pastries. "May I try something?"

Zeke leaped over to the table and handed the principal a plate. "Of course! May I interest you in a strawberry scone?"

"Sure," he said. "Thank you."

Gabriella carried the box of plaques in and set them down by Martha. "I have all the awards for the teachers," she whispered to her.

"Great," Martha replied quietly. "I gave the list to Sharpay. She'll give them out." She glanced over at Sharpay as she set up her microphone. "At least I hope she will. Do you think she'll keep to the script that I wrote for her?"

Gabriella noticed Martha's worried expression. "No one loves the spotlight more than Sharpay. I'm sure she'll do fine!"

The cafeteria started to fill up as more and more seniors and faculty members arrived.

Everyone was happy to have a delicious breakfast, hear the music, and hang out with their friends. Soon, the entire senior class and all their teachers were chatting and eating happily.

Just then a loud voice boomed over the portable P.A. "Good morning everyone!" Sharpay sang out. "Welcome to our awesome Senior Breakfast!"

Everyone looked over at Sharpay. Martha had to hand it to her, the girl definitely knew how to get people to pay attention. The chattering in the room quieted down, and everyone turned to face Sharpay.

"I've been given the privilege of announcing this year's teachers' awards," she said. "This has been a great year, and we all owe tremendous thanks to our wonderful teachers, who continue to inspire us. Without them, we would never have become the students that we are today."

All the seniors applauded.

Martha leaned over to Taylor. "So far, she's staying close to the script I gave her," she whispered.

Taylor held up her crossed fingers. She was never sure what Sharpay would do next. But to Taylor's amazement, Sharpay delivered all three plaques as instructed. Ms. Darbus, Coach Bolton, and Principal Matsui received plaques from the senior class. After the awards had been given out, Sharpay cued the band. They played a swing medley that soon had everyone up on their feet and dancing.

"And let's hear it for the chair of this phenomenal breakfast, Ms. Martha Cox!" the lead saxophone player shouted at the end of the set. He stood up and pointed across the room at Martha.

Martha stood up and took a bow. "Thanks to all of you!" she told the crowd. "You're all the best. I hope that everyone had a really great time. I know I did. This is one of the best moments of senior year! Wildcats forever!"

Gabriella was standing with Troy, clapping for her friend. But she couldn't help noticing that Taylor and Chad were standing at opposite

166

sides of the cafeteria. This isn't good, Gabriella thought. She knew Chad felt really bad about what had happened. She hoped that Chad would at least try to write Taylor a senior note . . . and they would all get back to being friends!

CHAPTER
FOURTEEN

Sharpay flipped the switches on the wall and saw the Wellington Community Center's stage light up. The backdrop that Martha and the other Wildcats had painted was illuminated by six large floodlights hanging high over the stage. The scenery looked amazing. Sharpay had to hand it to Martha and the others, who had all stayed up late the night before to finish painting the set. They had really come through with delivering the scenery. The backdrop's starry night sky would be the perfect background for the musical numbers the show included. Taking a deep breath, Sharpay steadied herself for the day's rehearsal. This was the big one! Today was the dress rehearsal.

Sharpay loved dress rehearsals. Everyone was in full costume and the show ran as if it were opening night. The lights, the makeup, the costumes—it was showtime! As she walked down the aisle, Sharpay grinned. She was proud of the work that she had done. The show was going to be great. Being a director was not the same as being the star of the show, but calling the shots and telling people what to do? Well, that was certainly something that Sharpay realized she was *very* good at doing.

"Hey, Sharpay!" Ryan called as he rushed down the aisle. "It's almost curtain time! Are you ready?"

Sharpay settled into her seat in the middle of the third row. She dug her clipboard out of her bag, ready to take the final notes that she would give the cast and crew after the rehearsal. Having been through many dress rehearsals, she knew the importance of these last-minute notes from the director. It was the director's responsibility to correct any mistakes that might happen during the run-through so that the show would be perfect on opening night.

"I'm ready," Sharpay told her brother confidently. "Let's hope the cast and crew are ready, too."

"Oh, we're ready," Hannah said, walking by with Carly trailing right behind her. Carly was having a hard time walking with two large garment bags slung over her shoulder. In her other hand she was carting a small suitcase that had Hannah's name written on it in gold glitter.

"You need some help?" Ryan asked as he saw Carly struggling. He hurried over and took the garment bags from her. He noted the stickers on the bags. "Are these both Hannah's costumes? Where are yours?"

"Oh, I have to go back and get mine," Carly said. "I couldn't carry everything."

Ryan raised his eyebrows as he watched Hannah prance over to Sharpay. Clearly, Hannah was learning some theater tips from his twin sister! He rolled his eyes and then turned his focus back to Carly. "Don't worry," he said. "I'll bring these up to the dressing room. You should be responsible for your own costume, not your sister's."

Carly's eyes opened wide. "Really?" she asked hopefully. "That would be great, because I'd like to have a chance to run through my own lines before the curtain goes up." She smiled at Ryan. "Thank you!"

"No problem," Ryan told her. "Glad that I could help you out." He shook his head as he watched Carly skip back up the aisle to get her own costume.

"Are you all set?" Sharpay asked Hannah as she sat down next to her.

"Yes," Hannah said, flipping her long blond

hair over one shoulder. Sharpay raised her eyebrows. Wow, she thought. Hannah is turning out to be quite a pro!

As Ryan made his way up the stage steps, he took a double take. With Hannah sitting next to his sister, the resemblance was remarkable. That's all this show needs, he thought to himself—another Sharpay! He rocked his head back and forth in his hand, silently hoping that all would go well for this run-through.

"Looks like we've got two Sharpays, huh?" Kelsi commented. She was standing in the wings of the stage looking out into the audience.

"Seems that way." Ryan sighed as he walked by her. "Let's hope that she hasn't learned *all* of my sister's bad habits."

Kelsi laughed. "I'll hope that with all my fingers *and* toes crossed!"

Max dashed across the stage and slid to a stop in front of Kelsi and Ryan. "We've got trouble," he said, panting. He put his hands on his knees, bending his head down to try to catch his breath.

"What's wrong?" Kelsi asked. Max was the stage manager for the production. She took his hand. "Breathe, Max," she instructed. "And tell us what's going on."

"It's Rosie," Max said worriedly. "She says that she can't be in the show!" He looked up at Ryan and Kelsi. "And she's the lead in the best number. The finale! Without her, the show is doomed!"

"Oh, I can do that number," Hannah cooed from the audience. She was listening very carefully to the discussion, and when she heard that Rosie might not perform, she seemed to take it as a great sign. "I know that song perfectly."

Everyone turned to look at Hannah, who was beaming as she sprang up onto the stage. She stood at center stage and sang a few notes from Rosie's song. All eyes went to Sharpay. As the director, she was the one who would ultimately make the decision.

Sharpay stood up from her seat. She lifted her

eyes up to the bright lights over the stage. What would Ms. Darbus do in this situation? she thought. She closed her eyes and tried to imagine that she was her cool, confident teacher. Her teacher who was a seasoned director and always knew what to do. When Sharpay opened her eyes, she had her answer. Slowly, she climbed the steps to the stage.

"Hannah, practice the song with Kelsi and get ready to go on in case Rosie doesn't show," she instructed. Once they had left the stage, she turned to Max. "Max, go get Troy and tell him about Rosie. He'll talk some sense into her." She shooed him away with one hand.

Ryan grinned at Sharpay. "Good call. You know what Ms. Darbus always says?"

Looking up at her brother, Sharpay said, "The show must go on?"

"No," Ryan said, shaking his head. "A bad dress rehearsal means a great show!"

"Let's hope so," Sharpay said anxiously. "That Rosie was my ace in the hole for the finale.

What is it with these basketball players? They are so full of *drama*!" She turned on her heel and huffed back down to her director's seat. She only hoped that the sage old words of the theater gods would prove true and that this bad dress rehearsal would lead to a stellar opening night.

Troy peered through the small window on the gymnasium door and then nodded his head. "Yup, she's in there," he said to Gabriella. "Just as I thought."

"No better place to clear your head than the court, huh?" Gabriella said. When Max ran to find them and let them know what was happening, Troy knew right away where they'd find Rosie. "Do you want me to stay out here?"

"I think you should come with me," Troy told her. "You always know the right thing to say." He took her hand and opened the door. "I don't know what to say to her. I thought that she was going to be fine after our talk yesterday."

"She's going through a hard time," Gabriella

whispered to him. "You just need to speak from your heart. You'll find the right things to say to her."

Jogging over to the edge of the court, Troy reached out and grabbed the basketball as it rebounded from the rim. "Watch your follow-through," he said as he passed the ball back to Rosie.

Rosie caught the ball and dribbled it a few times before setting up her shot at the free-throw line again. She didn't say a word. She just let the ball fly from her hands, right into the basket.

"Nice shot," Troy called as he reached up for the ball. "So what are you doing here, Rosie?" he said, passing the ball back to her. "Aren't you supposed to be at the dress rehearsal?"

Taking her time, Rosie just concentrated on the ball in her hand. She didn't look up or respond. Troy grew concerned and looked over at Gabriella, who was sitting on the lowest bench of the bleachers. She shrugged and signaled for

Troy to try again. Not knowing quite what to do next, Troy just took Gabriella's advice. He spoke from his heart.

"You know, Rosie," he began. "Whenever I am faced with a decision, I always feel that the court helps me to focus. I've put in a lot of time at the foul line." He smiled as he pointed to the red stripe by Rosie's feet. "There's nothing like shooting some hoops to help you make a decision."

Rosie held the ball at her hip and tilted her head. She gazed at Troy and narrowed her eyes. "You do this, too?" she asked.

"Of course," he said, pushing his bangs away from his eyes. "I always come to the court to think." He moved a little closer to her. "Rosie, do you want to talk about it?" He waited a moment and then continued. "You didn't talk to your parents about the show, did you?"

Opening her eyes wide, Rosie shook her head. "How'd you know?" she asked.

"Well," Troy said carefully, "if you *had* talked

to them, I don't think you'd be hiding out in here instead of being onstage at the dress rehearsal, where you're supposed to be right now."

Rosie looked down at her feet, and her shoulders slumped. "I just can't tell them. I mean, they'll be shocked! And I don't think they are going to understand. They'll think it's silly that I want to be onstage."

"Not when they hear you sing," Gabriella said, getting up from her seat. "Rosie, you have such a talent. They will be so proud of you for being part of the musical. *And* being part of the basketball team. You don't have to choose between them."

"Believe me," Troy said, laughing, "that's the hard part. But as we've explained, you don't have to choose. You can be a singing star *and* a basketball star at the same time."

Rosie looked back and forth between Troy and Gabriella. She smiled. "Okay, okay. I'll listen to you guys finally."

Troy laughed. He grabbed the ball away from

Rosie and did a perfect layup. "Cool," he told her.

"Okay, well," Rosie began, "I'm going to head over to rehearsal now . . . after I make a quick call home. I want to make sure that my parents are going to be here tomorrow night to see my debut . . . as a singing basketball star!"

"Nice!" Troy cheered.

"We can't wait," Gabriella added.

As Rosie ran out of the gym, Troy passed the ball to Gabriella. "Want to try a little one on one?" he asked, already moving into an offensive position.

"You know, I might be a singing basketball star, too," Gabriella joked.

"An academic ace student who sings *and* plays basketball?" he said, joking.

Just then, Gabriella let the ball in her hand fly, and they both watched it swish through the net. Gabriella bowed as she giggled. "Oh, you know it!" she said coyly. She snatched the ball and ran off down the court, but Troy was too quick for her.

"Out of bounds, Montez!" he called.

They both laughed and headed back to the stage to watch the dress rehearsal. Their work on the court was done.

CHAPTER FIFTEEN

The next day, Gabriella and Troy were headed to the Wellington Community Center after school, maybe for the last time. Gabriella felt a little sad. Today she would teach her last swimming lesson, and later that night the kids would perform the musical. The senior project was coming to an end.

"Hey coach, are you ready for the last swimming lesson?" Troy asked Gabriella as he pulled into the parking lot.

"Yes," Gabriella said. "I'm really hoping that Henry puts his head in the water today. He's made so much progress over the last few weeks, but that would be huge!"

Troy smiled at Gabriella. "Well, if anyone can get him to do that, it's you," he said, giving her hand a squeeze.

"Is the team ready for the big game tomorrow?" Gabriella asked as she walked with Troy to the community center's entrance. She knew that the Wildcats had been working hard to get the basketball team in shape.

"I think they are," Troy said thoughtfully. "They have a really good chance of winning. It will be a good game."

After making a plan to meet up after practice, Gabriella slipped into the locker room to change. As she stood in front of her locker, she thought about senior year and how everything was going by so quickly. She wanted to slow time down so she could enjoy all her friends and the best moments of senior year.

When she walked into the pool area, she expected to see Henry sitting on the side with his feet dangling in the water. But Henry wasn't there. Gabriella gasped. Had he not shown up for the last class? She scanned the bleachers and then the pool, looking for Henry's dark hair and bright red swim goggles.

Suddenly, Gabriella spotted him. Henry was already in the pool! He was in the area that was used for free swim before the class began. He was happily playing around with some other kids in the class.

"Hi, Gabriella!" Henry called as soon as he spotted her.

Gabriella beamed with pride. She was so excited that he was already in the pool. The progress he had made here at the center was unbelievable. Gabriella was grinning from ear to ear as she walked over to him.

"Hey there, Henry!" she exclaimed.

"I've been waiting for you!" Henry responded.

"Great," Gabriella said. "I'm excited to see

you. And you look like you're having a good time!"

Henry smiled and then went back to playing with his friends. Mr. Hall walked up and gave Gabriella a tap on her shoulder.

"Well done, Ms. Montez," he said, winking at her. "I don't think that we would have gotten Henry near the water if it hadn't been for you. Thank you for all you've done for him, and for everyone else at the center. I know that the head of the center, Mr. Davis, is going to thank all the seniors from East High for all their hard work later, after the show, but I had to give you my personal thanks. I know that doing the East High senior project here at the center was your idea."

Gabriella blushed and looked down at her feet. "Well, this has been really fun," she told the swim teacher. "Swimming has always been a part of my life and I was happy to share the sport with these kids." She looked over at the pool. "Especially with Henry! He's come so far since the beginning of the class."

"I know," Mr. Hall replied, grinning widely. He blew his whistle and announced to the kids that class was about to begin.

Jumping into the water, Gabriella hoped that Henry would be all right with the first exercise of the day. Mr. Hall had planned on the swimmers using the kickboards and putting their faces in the water. She watched carefully as Henry grabbed a board. He looked over at her.

"I can do this now," he said with confidence. "Just like Rufus!"

Gabriella watched with delight as Henry kicked his way across the pool with his face in the water. The huge grin on his face at the end of the lap was no match for Gabriella's own smile. Henry had done it!

"All right, Henry!" she called, clapping her hands above her head. "You did it!"

"I did it!" Henry echoed. "That was so much fun," he added.

Gabriella waded over to him. "I'm so glad to hear you say that," she said. "I hope that you'll keep swimming. You will be a great swimmer one day."

"Thanks," Henry told her. "I bet I can swim faster than Rufus now!"

Gabriella giggled and ruffled Henry's wet hair. "I'm sure you could."

Sharpay paced around the backstage area. She was clutching a clipboard and wearing a headset, barking orders into the mouthpiece.

"One of the stage-left sidelights is not on," she reported as she did her final check of the stage lights. "Hello?" She adjusted the microphone on her headset. "Hello? Zeke, are you there?" she said a little louder.

The light suddenly snapped on and lit up the stage. Sharpay smiled. "Thank you," she said, squinting into the dark theater. She gave a little wave and then turned her attention back to her clipboard. A director's to-do list on opening night was endless. Being the director was really hard work!

"Oh, Sharpay!" Ms. Darbus gushed as she came over to her with arms wide. "You look like a true director!" She pointed to Sharpay's headset and clipboard. "I'm so excited to see what you kids have done here."

Sharpay gave Ms. Darbus an air kiss on each cheek. "Thank you!" She smoothed the front of her satin fuchsia dress. "Opening night!" she sang out. "Everyone's excited!" She flashed her teacher an award-winning smile.

"Indeed," Ms. Darbus replied, beaming. She took a step back and eyed Sharpay. "You're very calm, Sharpay. Keep up the good work." She gave her an approving nod. "I'll be in the audience. Break a leg! And I'll see you after the show!"

As soon as her teacher walked away, Sharpay exhaled. That was probably some of my best acting ever! she thought. Sharpay was actually a nervous wreck. She didn't want to let on to Ms. Darbus how she was really feeling. A director should never let the audience know the craziness happening behind the curtain!

"The cast is waiting for you," Ryan said, coming up behind his sister. "They're all sitting in the dressing room. Everyone looks very nervous. You should give them a Ms. Darbus speech."

"Should I go get her? She's here," Sharpay replied, turning to run after her teacher.

Ryan shook his head and reached out to grab her shoulders. "Not her, *you!*" He took both of Sharpay's hands in his and looked her in the eye. "Sharpay, *you're* the director," he said calmly. "The cast wants to hear from *you*. You know Ms. Darbus always gives one of her inspiring talks right before the curtain. The director has to set the tone for the show. You've got to go talk to the cast."

Sharpay knew that Ryan was right. As the director, she knew it was her responsibility to give the talk. Sharpay had always loved Ms. Darbus's talks before a show. She'd ask everyone to speak while passing an old prop that she had kept from a show she had worked on long ago. The prop reminded Sharpay of a magic wand,

and she always felt that to hold it before a show brought good luck. She gathered her thoughts, and took a pink scarf from her bag. She hoped it would do the trick. She marched into the dressing room area to find her cast.

When she walked into the room, she saw all their faces turn to her. And they all looked pretty nervous, too. She took a deep breath.

"This is it!" she exclaimed. "This is opening night. We did it!" she cheered. "Putting on a show takes teamwork. And everyone here is a part of the team." She looked around at the kids and held up her scarf. "This is a scarf that I wore during one of my first shows. Before a show, it's nice to have each cast member hold the scarf and speak. It's a good-luck ritual."

Hannah quickly grabbed the scarf. Holding it close to her face, she sighed. "Oh, I hope that this gives me luck! I'm so nervous!"

"Don't say that!" Max warned. "Theater people always say 'Break a leg'—not 'Good luck'! You don't want to jinx us, do you?"

Hannah glared at Max. "Whatever," she said. "I'm just glad that it's opening night and that *I* have the first solo."

Rolling her eyes, Rosie took the scarf next. "I'm just happy to be here," she said. "And I'm glad that my parents are in the audience."

The scarf continued around the cast circle. Ryan winked at Sharpay. She had really come through and had proven herself to be a very good director. He looked down at his watch. "Okay, people, we've got to wrap this up. The audience is waiting!"

Clapping her hands, Sharpay nodded her head. "Now go out there and sing your hearts out!"

The cast cheered, and then everyone scattered to take their places. The show was about to begin!

"Here we go," Sharpay announced. She hugged her clipboard nervously and settled in backstage to watch the show.

Gabriella sat in the audience next to Taylor.

Most of the other Wildcats were helping out on the stage crew, running lights and sound. Gabriella and Taylor had helped out with makeup and costumes, so now they could enjoy the show.

"Hi, Sue!" Taylor called out. Sue was walking down the aisle with her mom, looking for seats.

"Hi, Taylor," Sue said, waving.

Sue's mother smiled at Taylor and came over to where she was seated. "It is so nice to meet you!" she gushed. "Sue talks about you all the time."

Taylor blushed and stood up to shake Sue's mom's hand. She was so proud of Sue, and she had loved working with her on trivia questions. Finding that she and Sue had a love of trivia in common had made the whole experience of volunteering even more special. "Oh, thank you," she said. "We've had a good time. Right, Sue?"

Sue nodded her head up and down. Then she tugged on her mom's hand, telling her they had to get seats.

"Well, it was nice to meet you," Sue's mom said, walking away.

"See?" Gabriella said. "You really made a difference. Sue looked so happy! Way to go, Taylor!" She watched Sue and her mom sit down, then caught sight of some other people who they knew. A couple of rows in front of them, Chad was sitting with Jason. He kept turning around, hoping to catch Taylor's eye, but Taylor just ignored him.

"Come on, Taylor," Gabriella said as she saw Chad waving. "I know you see him."

"Huh?" Taylor said innocently. She was trying very hard not to engage in any conversation with—or about—Chad. Senior notes would be delivered tomorrow morning, and she knew that he had not purchased one. "What do you mean?" she asked coyly.

Gabriella shrugged. When Taylor made a decision, it was impossible to change her mind! At least tomorrow the notes will be delivered and this cold frost will end, thought Gabriella. Or at least she *hoped* it would end. She wondered if Chad had taken her advice and written Taylor a senior note.

"Hi, Gabriella!" Henry called out. He was walking down the aisle with his dad and brought him over to say hello.

"Nice to meet you," Henry's dad said. He leaned over and shook her hand.

Gabriella noticed that Henry's father had the same bright blue eyes as his son. She looked down at Henry and smiled.

"Thank you for helping Henry," Henry's dad said. "I hear that he's a swimmer now." He pulled Henry closer to him.

"We had a lot of fun, right, Henry?" Gabriella said, grinning.

"Definitely," Henry said with a shy smile.

Just then, Kelsi walked out onstage. Henry and his father took their seats as the audience quieted down. Kelsi took her place at the piano in the orchestra pit just in front of the stage. She nodded to members of the East High band who were playing in the orchestra, then she counted out the beat.

The show moved along without a hitch. Everyone made their entrances perfectly on cue. When Rosie came onstage, a hush fell over the crowd as she began to sing. Her voice was so clear and powerful. Just like Troy, who was so much fun to watch onstage, Gabriella thought as she watched Rosie's performance. Rosie was a natural. She came alive on the stage, and her finale brought the house down!

During the curtain call, Kelsi went over to the wings and grabbed James and brought him out to center stage to take a bow. She pointed to him. "Ladies and gentlemen, the composer of our songs for this performance was Mr. James Connelly!"

Everyone applauded wildly, especially those onstage. James looked embarrassed but happy. He took his bow and waved to everyone before disappearing in the wings.

At the end of the curtain call, Mr. Davis, the

director of the community center, grabbed the microphone.

"Thank you all for coming today," he said. "I'd like to thank all the East High Wildcats for helping out here at the center for the last month. Your involvement here has meant so much to all the kids and the staff as well, from the new mural in the game room to the show we've just seen, and the big basketball game scheduled for tomorrow!"

The audience roared and cheered. Gabriella and Taylor shared a look, knowing that their senior project was more important than they could have ever imagined. It was a true shining moment for all the Wildcats.

CHAPTER SIXTEEN

Wylie Wildcat slid into Ms. Darbus's homeroom, holding a basket of red envelopes. He did a dance as the classroom full of seniors clapped along enthusiastically. Some people even got up to dance with him. Even Ms. Darbus got into the Wildcat groove. She grabbed Wylie's paw when he danced over to her. With a flourish, he swung her around in a lavish ballroom twirl. Ms. Darbus laughed as she spun around. Dancing with the Wildcat mascot was the perfect way to begin any day!

Taylor tried to get the class to pay attention. "All right, everyone," she yelled. "Wylie has some other homerooms to visit this morning, so if everyone would please take their seats, we'll hand out the senior notes."

Taylor was feeling a bit on edge this morning. Even though she was trying her best to hide her feelings, she couldn't deny that she was disappointed. Seeing everyone else get their senior notes was hard, especially when she knew that there wasn't one in that basket for her from Chad. She had checked the list of the seniors who had purchased notes, and there was only one name missing from the list. Taylor couldn't believe that Chad hadn't gotten her a note. Trying not to let her feelings show, she forced a smile as Ryan romped around in his Wildcat outfit.

Troy looked over at Gabriella and winked. He was never one for writing down his feelings, but writing his note to Gabriella had been easy.

He couldn't wait for her to see what he had written.

Smiling back at Troy, Gabriella knew that he'd love what she had written in her senior note to him. She was happy to have a chance to tell Troy how much he meant to her, and how much fun she was having senior year. But her happiness seemed to evaporate when she caught sight of Taylor. Gabriella could see that her friend's face was strained. She had written Taylor a senior note, but she knew that hers wasn't the one that Taylor was hoping for. Taylor was trying to put on a good show, but Gabriella couldn't help but notice the sad look in her eyes. Scanning the room, Gabriella couldn't find Chad. She hoped that in Wylie's basket there was a note for Taylor from him! She didn't like seeing the two of them not speaking to each other.

One by one, all their friends got their notes. Sharpay sat happily reading all her "fan mail," as she called it. Martha giggled when she read hers, and even Jason and Zeke seemed pretty happy with the notes that Wylie handed them.

When the last envelope had been delivered, there was a knock at Ms. Darbus's door. Through the glass, everyone saw that Chad was standing there—dressed in a red tuxedo jacket and holding a bunch of red-and-white balloons!

Ms. Darbus opened the door and smiled at Chad. Gabriella was sure that their teacher was in on the surprise. Otherwise she would definitely have written Chad up for being late, Gabriella mused.

"Taylor McKessie!" Chad announced as he walked into the classroom. "I have a special delivery for you."

Everyone in the class stood still and became silent. They all watched as Chad got down on one knee and handed Taylor a red envelope with a red rose attached.

"But . . . but . . . you never bought a note," Taylor stuttered.

Chad just grinned. "As far as *you* know," he said. He held up his thumb to Troy, who was looking rather pleased with himself. He turned back to gaze up at Taylor. "I might have had someone else purchase the note to throw you off. You know, a secret play."

Gabriella brought her hands up to her chest and sighed. This was one of the sweetest gestures that Chad had ever made! And it seemed to be working. Taylor was beaming. She took the envelope and read the note. The tension between the two of them had definitely cleared. The whole class erupted into loud applause.

Troy slapped Chad on the back. "Sweet," he said. "Good job, bro!"

Chad laughed as he squeezed Taylor's shoulder. "Thanks, man," he said to Troy.

"You knew all about this, huh?" Gabriella said, playfully shoving Troy.

"Yup," Troy said, grinning. "Top secret game plan comes through in the clutch!" he exclaimed, reaching over for a high five with Chad.

"And now it's time for a party," Sharpay said, extending her hand to present another envelope.

Only this one was hot pink. "Ryan and I are having a pre-graduation party at the country club this weekend. Hope you can make it. Toodles!" She spun on the heel of her pink mule and continued to hand out the invites to her classmates.

"Wow," Chad said as he read the invitation to himself. Back to the Lava Springs Country Club? he thought. Hmm. Thinking about all the kitchen time he had logged there the summer before senior year didn't really make him want to return. His hands were still recovering from washing all those dirty dishes.

Gabriella stepped in. "Are you kidding?" she asked. She looked around at her friends. "This is an invitation to a party, not a job offer. This will be fun."

Shaking her head, Taylor smiled. "It's from *Sharpay*, Gabriella. You never know what she's up to."

Troy tapped the invite in the palm of his hand. "I don't know," he said. "I think this really is like

201

a gesture of goodwill. Sharpay was great last night. She really pulled off directing the show for those kids."

Gabriella nodded. "True," she said. "Rosie was amazing. I hope that she keeps up her singing."

"Wait until you see her out on the court!" Troy added. "The big game is tonight! Southside beware. The Wellington Warriors are coming to town!"

Chad reached over to slap a high five with Troy. "They are going to rock it out tonight. With all the plays we taught them, I know that they will win."

Across the room, Ryan took off his Wylie headgear for a moment. He took a sip of water from a water bottle.

"Everyone is buzzing about the party, Sharpay," Ryan said to his sister when she came over to him.

"I know," she said with a grin. She clapped her hands excitedly. Then she leaned in closer to him. "Finally, I'll be back in the spotlight! Daddy said the new outdoor stage is almost finished. I can't *wait* to perform again."

"I know," Ryan said, rolling his eyes. "So I've heard. And heard again."

Sharpay sighed heavily. "I mean being a director was great and all, but I need to be back onstage. *Center* stage." She dramatically put her hands to her heart. "My people demand it. I cannot deny the public their fair share of *me*." She stopped and flashed her brother a wide grin. "Stephan Kingston, the new pianist at the club, has arranged a perfect number for me." She caught Ryan's eye. "I mean, for *us*, if you want to join me."

Laughing, Ryan shook his head. "Oh, no," he said. "This performance is all you."

When Taylor spotted Ryan taking a break, she darted over to him.

"Come on, Wildcat," she scolded. "We have a few more homerooms to visit before the bell rings."

Ryan obediently slid the head of his costume back on. He followed Taylor toward the door to continue with his delivery duties.

"Bye, Wylie!" the class called out.

Taylor took the Wildcat's paw and led the mascot out of the room. Before leaving, she turned around at the door and winked at Chad. Chad waved, relieved that the tension between them was over. Phew, he thought. That was definitely a close one!

There was a rumble of cheering coming from the gymnasium that made Troy's heart race. The Wildcat cheerleaders had come to warm up the crowd before the Wellington Community Center game. Troy knew that the players were all nervous and excited. This was it!

The team was sitting in the locker room just minutes before the game was to start. Troy looked over at Chad. They had planned what they were going to say to the team earlier. Troy's dad's speeches always inspired the Wildcats to give their best. Troy just hoped that he'd be able to psych the team up the way his dad always did.

Rosie sat on the bench watching Troy, waiting for the cue to run into the gym. She was wearing a new team uniform donated by the Evans family. Being part of a real team gave her a great feeling. Last night before the musical she had been nervous—but today she was just excited. She felt at home on the court and she wasn't scared at all. There was no solo here tonight. Everything now was all about teamwork.

"Okay, team," Troy said, getting everyone's attention. "Here's the moment that you've all been waiting for—game time!"

The team let out a cheer, and Troy nodded his head.

"Yes, it's game time," he repeated. "But what you have to remember is all the skills we learned in practice. Pass the ball around, look out for one another, and be a team."

"What's our name?" Chad cheered, leaping

off the bench. He pumped his arm in the air as he waited for the response. "I said," he bellowed, "what's our name?"

"Wellington!" the team roared back. They stood up and ran toward the locker-room door. It was game time!

As the team passed through the locker-room door, Troy and Chad slapped a high five with each player before they rushed out onto the court. The crowd, made up of East High seniors and friends and family of the team, was loud and enthusiastic as the team set up for their warm-up. Zeke and Jason were standing under the net, keeping the warm-up moving by passing balls back to the players. Each team member did a couple of layup shots and then lined up to do free throws.

As Troy walked into the gym, he looked up into the crowded bleachers. He spotted Gabriella right away. She was holding up a sign for the team. She was sitting next to her mom, and on the other side of her were Troy's parents.

Coach Bolton stood up, clapping wildly. When he saw Troy looking at him, he raised his fist high in a thumbs-up.

Feeling pumped up, Troy clapped his hands together and huddled with his team. "It's game time, Warriors! Let's show this place what you can do."

The buzzer sounded and the game started. Rosie won the tip-off, so Wellington had the ball to start. The other team had a few advantages, including some tall players, but Troy noticed right away that they weren't playing as a team. He knew that to win games, everyone had to work together.

The minutes ticked away, and the baskets added up on the scoreboard. It was a close game, and when halftime came, the score was tied. Back in the locker room, Troy and Chad shared a look. They knew that this pep talk had to be good. There was so much nervous energy in the room. They had to channel that energy and help focus the team.

"We're so close!" one of the players said, slumping down on the bench.

"Number twenty-three is so tall! Did you see that guy? Is he in high school or something?" another player blurted out.

Troy held up his hands for quiet. "I know it's tough out there, and you guys have been doing so well. Did you see the score? You weren't even on the schedule to play a month ago!"

The team grew quiet. They knew that what Troy was saying was true.

"Now we've got to take the lead and then hold on to it," he advised. "And you can do that. Just stay in the game. And remember our team play book."

"We've been watching the other team," Chad added. "They aren't passing the ball and playing like a team. You can beat them. Come on, Wellington Warriors! Let's see you play!"

The cheering in the locker room got louder. Everyone was pumped up and ready to head back out to the court. Rosie passed through the locker room door last.

"Even if we don't win," Rosie said, looking up at Troy, "thank you for making us feel like a team."

Troy smiled and put his arm around her. "We are a team. A good team. Now go out there and make your team a *winning* team!"

Troy watched as Rosie jogged out on the court. Just as his dad did at all *his* games, Troy paced back and forth in front of the team bench. Everyone looked as if they were having fun, and he was glad about that. More than anything, he wanted the kids at the center to enjoy basketball as much as he did. Win or lose, they'd know what it was like to play as a team. And nothing was better than that.

In the final seconds of the game, number twenty-three sank a basket, pulling Southside ahead by two points. Troy looked up at the stands and saw his dad. He knew what he had to do. He called a time-out.

The team huddled around Troy. He gazed into the faces of his young team. Then he glanced up at the scoreboard. There were twelve seconds left on the clock.

"Team, this is game time," he said. He took a deep breath, waiting for everyone in the huddle to take the moment in. "When the Wildcats played West High the last time, we ran into this exact situation. We were really nervous, but we pulled through. I know you can do it."

Chad pulled out a chalkboard and sketched out the play. Everyone focused on the board, studying the play.

"Okay," Troy said, "who wants the ball?"

Everyone in the huddle pointed to Rosie. She looked down at the ground and then slowly lifted her eyes to meet Troy's gaze. "I can do it," she said. "Get me the ball."

Everyone put their hands in the circle. "Go-oo-o-o-o team!" they all chanted.

The Wellington Warriors had paid attention during all their practices. They moved the ball swiftly down the court and made sure Rosie got the ball. As she set up for the shot, number twenty-three jumped up to block her. He stepped in front and bumped her just as she released the ball from her hand. The referee's hand went up. The clock ran out, and the buzzer sounded.

"Foul!" The referee yelled.

Rosie was knocked to the ground and looked up just in time to see the ball hit the backboard, roll around the rim, and then drop in. *Swish!* Two points! The game was tied!

Over the cheers, the referee added, "And one!"

Rosie searched for Troy on the sidelines. She would have to stand at the foul line and shoot not only for the foul, but to win the game!

The crowd went crazy! Troy ran out on the court and grabbed Rosie. In a flash, he was by her side, helping her up.

"Don't think about anything except that ball and that net," Troy instructed her. "Block everything else out. It's just you and the ball, Rosie. You can do this."

He rushed off the court and held his breath along with everyone else in the gym. Rosie took her time. She bounced the ball a few times in front of her before lifting it up for the shot. After she let the ball go, she squeezed her eyes shut tightly.

The loud roar of the crowd let her know that the ball was in! Suddenly Rosie was swept up on Zeke's shoulders and paraded around the court. They had won the game!

Troy could not have been happier. He was so proud of his team, and Rosie. He knew she could do it!

Mr. Davis came up behind him. "Thank you and to all the Wildcats," he told him. "This senior project has given so much to our kids here. This win is only part of the celebration."

"It's been really amazing volunteering here at the center," Troy said, taking in the scene around him. All the Wildcats were celebrating. It was nice to look around and recognize so many of the kids from the center. Everyone looked so happy. He caught Gabriella's eye. She was beaming with pride.

Troy looked over at Mr. Davis and smiled. "We're going to miss these kids a lot. This has been one of the best things about senior year. It's been awesome," he said.

Mr. Davis reached out to shake Troy's hand. "Please come and visit anytime," he said. "It's been a pleasure."

Troy grinned. This was a moment he would never forget.

CHAPTER SEVENTEEN

Sharpay looked out the window of her bedroom. How could this be? she wondered as she held the drapes back. She had thought of every detail of the graduation party, from the napkin colors to the luau theme—not to mention the perfect dance routine she had specially choreographed for her debut on the new outdoor stage at the club. She had thought of everything and was unbelievably prepared. Except for one thing. Rain!

As the rain continued to beat down, Sharpay watched her muddled reflection in the window.

"Everything is ruined!" she blurted out.

"Oh, Sharpay," Ryan said when he walked into her room and saw his sister's pouting face. "Come on, it's just a little rain."

Sharpay turned around and stared at her twin. She narrowed her eyes to a laser glare. "What? A *little* rain? Look at it!" she cried, pointing at the torrential downpour outside. "There's a tropical rainstorm happening out there!" She flung herself facedown on her queen-size bed, burying her head deep into one of its many pink silk pillows.

"Okay, so there's a little rain," Ryan conceded. He walked over to the window to inspect the weather. "But you know the Wildcats, nothing can dampen their spirits!" He clapped his hands together, trying to snap his sister out of her funk. "Come on, where's your inner actress? Where's the star performer?" He reached over and poked her. "It's showtime!" He flashed his hands in front of his face, extending all his fingers to form perfect jazz hands.

Rolling over on her back, Sharpay draped her arm dramatically over her eyes. "Oh, and let's not even *think* about what my hair will look like in this humidity!" She rolled back on her stomach to hide her face again. "Oh, everything is ruined!"

Ryan shrugged. He knew there was nothing he could say that would change Sharpay's mood. He'd have to let her wallow there for a while. Before he left, he tried one more time. "You thought everything was ruined at the center, too," he said. "And see how that turned out." When he didn't get a response, Ryan shook his head sadly and walked out of his sister's room.

After the door clicked shut, Sharpay lifted her head. Suddenly, she had a brilliant idea. The outdoor luau that she had envisioned could be moved *inside*—she'd delegate that move to Mr. Fulton at the club. She jumped out of her bed and grabbed her sparkly pink cell phone. If this is going to happen, Sharpay thought, I better start moving!

After a few hours, even Ryan was getting nervous. Sharpay still had not moved from her room. Stephan Kingston, the pianist, was now calling Ryan on his cell phone because Sharpay wasn't picking up her phone. Stephan explained that he wanted to run through the performance one more time before the show, especially since Sharpay had made a few last-minute changes. Ryan wasn't sure what Stephan was talking about, but he promised to get Sharpay to the Lava Springs Country Club—quickly.

Just as Ryan was about to barge into her room, Sharpay appeared at the top of the stairs. She waltzed down the steps with her costume draped over her arm.

"The show has to go on, right?" she asked, flashing Ryan a smile.

"You know it!" Ryan replied, and jumped off the couch. "Dad called before to say that the crew has been working hard all day to move

217

the party inside to the ballroom." He walked over to Sharpay and dropped his arm around her shoulder. "It's going to be a good show. And everything is all set for the luau."

"Perfect," Sharpay said. Her hair was up in a French braid with decorative flowers pinned along the sides.

Ryan eyed his sister. "What made you change your mind?" he asked as he reached for his red cap.

"Well," Sharpay said thoughtfully. "This is going to be one of my last performances for East High. I didn't want to disappoint anyone. *Everyone's* coming to see me, after all." She winked at her brother. "And I have a few surprises to spice up the show."

"Hmmm," Ryan said as he slipped into Sharpay's pink convertible.

"You'll be in the show, too, of course," Sharpay said as she put the key in the ignition.

Eying his sister, Ryan wondered what Sharpay was up to now. He smiled to himself as he realized that Sharpay's motivation for planning the graduation party wasn't about celebrating the end of the senior project or their upcoming graduation, it was all about performing. Even the theme of the party—the Hawaiian luau—fit into her plan for the perfect show. "All right," Ryan said. He was thankful that Sharpay had snapped out of her funk. Besides, how could he turn down a chance to perform? He tilted his cap over his eyes as Sharpay drove to the country club.

The rain continued to pour down, pelting the roof of the car. Tapping out the beat on the dashboard with his fingers, Ryan thought about the party. He couldn't help but be excited about seeing Kelsi. Maybe he'd even get up the nerve to ask her to dance! Working with her at the center had been really fun, and he wanted to spend more time with her.

When Sharpay and Ryan arrived at the country club, she popped open her large pink umbrella before stepping out of the car. Ryan just made a run for it but didn't get too soaked. He shook off the rain as he walked inside. The staff was scurrying around, getting all the last minute details right. Mr. Fulton, the manager of the country club, came running over to Sharpay and Ryan as soon as they stepped inside.

"Miss Evans," he greeted her. He turned to Ryan. "And Mr. Evans." He bowed his head slightly and then continued. "I'm *so* sorry about this weather! But we've made all the adjustments that your father has asked for already. The ballroom has been altered and looks like a Hawaiian paradise! Come see!"

Mr. Fulton grabbed their hands and brought them to the ballroom doors. He took a dramatic pause before pulling the heavy doors open to reveal the elaborate decorations.

Sharpay gasped when she saw the room. The scene before her was incredible! There were large palm trees and bright colorful flowers everywhere. Onstage was a beautiful sunset backdrop. The staff had worked hard to transform the country-club ballroom into a tropical island—and it worked!

"Oh, this is beautiful," Sharpay cooed. She spun around happily. "It's just perfect! Absolutely perfect!" she squealed.

"Yes, I thought you'd say that," Mr. Fulton responded, gloating.

"Here's a new list that I need for the performance," Sharpay instructed. "Ryan and I will be in the dressing rooms until showtime."

"Yes, Ms. Evans," Mr. Fulton said dutifully. He took the list and looked over the requests. He didn't raise an eyebrow and then dashed off quickly.

While Sharpay and Ryan went to the dressing rooms to get ready, the rest of the Wildcats began to arrive. Ryan stuck his head out to see the room filling up. He had been right about the Wildcat spirit. Nothing could dampen the mood of all the seniors.

"This is unbelievable," Troy said as he walked into the ballroom. "Aloha!"

Gabriella clutched Troy's arm as she walked inside the room. "Wow, look at all the palm trees and the dancers in the grass skirts. Maybe I'll go get one, too!" She raced over to the table where a woman was handing them out.

"It might be raining outside, but in here it's sunny Hawaii!" Taylor exclaimed when she saw all the decorations. "Mmmm, do you think that there's some coconut over there?" Taylor stood on her toes and held on to Chad's shoulder to get a better view. She pointed to a table that had platters of food spread out across it. "There *is* fresh coconut!" she cried happily. "This really feels like Hawaii! Everything looks delicious."

"Wait until you try my coconut cake!" Zeke exclaimed from behind her. "When I heard the theme of this party, I was psyched. I've been wanting to make this cake for a long time. It's a good one. You'll have to try a slice."

"You can bet on that!" Chad replied enthusiastically, rubbing his stomach. He grinned at Taylor, happy that they were no longer not speaking. "I'm really glad that we came to the party together."

Taylor leaned over and hugged Chad. "Me, too."

Gabriella agreed. "I'm happy that *we're* all together!" she exclaimed.

"And no one has to wash the dishes!" Chad added. He looked over at the swinging doors that led to the kitchen. Memories of last summer came flooding back to him. He was definitely glad to be a guest, and not working!

"We all have a lot to celebrate," Troy said, looking at his friends. "The kids winning the basketball game, and everyone doing a great job at the community center. I'd say it was a banner senior project!"

Chad raised his fist in the air. "Three cheers for the East High senior class!"

All the seniors gathered around to give a loud roaring Wildcat cheer.

The music started and everyone moved to the dance floor. All the Wildcats were there to have a good time. Now that the senior project was over, there really wasn't much time left until the end of school. There'd be finals and prom— and then graduation.

"This party is rocking!" Jason exclaimed as he tried to keep up with Martha's dance moves.

Chad and Taylor danced over next to him. "And so are you, Wildcat!" Chad shouted as he pointed to Jason's new hip-hop moves. "You are jamming out here on the dance floor."

Jason laughed. He bowed to his partner. "Martha is an awesome teacher."

Grabbing Jason's hand, Martha pulled him to the front of the room. "Come on, let's get everyone to do the dance with us!"

Martha and Jason had everyone following their moves. They both made the steps look easy, and everyone joined in on the fun. Soon the whole crowd was dancing and moving to the beat of the music.

Gabriella glanced over at Troy. He was a great dancer, and she loved being out on the dance floor with him. She smiled and moved her arms and hips the same way Martha did at the front of the room.

When the song ended, everyone cheered and clapped.

"What's our name?" Chad cried.

"Wildcats!" the crowd responded.

Just then, the lights flickered on and off to get everyone's attention. Mr. Fulton stood on the stage, holding a microphone. "Hello, East High seniors," Mr. Fulton announced. "Welcome to your Hawaiian luau."

The cheers were so loud that Mr. Fulton had to quiet the crowd down first before continuing on with his speech. "Okay, okay," he said as the seniors settled down. "The Evans family is happy to have you all here today. And now, without further ado, I'd like to present a very special surprise for all of you. This musical number is dedicated to the seniors of East High. Please enjoy!"

"This should be interesting," Taylor whispered to Gabriella.

Before Gabriella could answer, the music swelled and Sharpay and Ryan appeared on the stage. Sharpay was wearing bright flowers in her hair, a sequined purple cropped top, and a grass skirt. Ryan was wearing white pants and a Hawaiian shirt that had large flowers all over it. Stephan, the country club pianist, began to play an upbeat tune. They paused at center stage for a moment and then began their song.

"Wow," Gabriella whispered to Taylor. "They went all out for this, huh?"

Taylor rolled her eyes. "Always!"

Much to everyone's surprise, Sharpay and Ryan were not alone onstage for long. The back curtain was lifted, and now dancing and singing along right beside them were Carly, Hannah, and Rosie! When the Wildcats recognized who was up onstage, there were loud cheers. The kids were fantastic. The crowd loved them!

Troy and Gabriella cheered the loudest. Gabriella couldn't wipe the wide grin off her face. Seeing all those kids perform made her so happy. She knew that the senior project was a huge success not only for the East High Wildcats but for the kids at the center, too.

When the song ended, everyone onstage held their final pose. The applause was deafening! Gabriella was so happy to see the kids get to do another performance and to be surrounded by all her friends. It was the perfect finale for the senior project. And the beginning of the end of a truly magical year.

Sharpay winked at Ryan. "Thanks," she said. "You gave me the perfect way to jazz up this number."

"And the crowd loves it!" Ryan replied. "Well done."

After the show, there was more dancing. Ryan got to dance with Kelsi, and Zeke was happy that Sharpay saved a dance for him.

Out on the dance floor, Troy whispered in Gabriella's ear. "I'm so proud of Rosie! And all the kids." He turned Gabriella around so that they were looking into each other's eyes. "Thank you, Gabriella. Thank you for making East High a special place, and for spreading that good feeling around—especially to all the kids at the community center."

Gabriella blushed and looked up at Troy. "You had a whole lot to do with that," she said with a smile. " All the Wildcats pulled through," she added. "This party is the perfect ending to the senior project."

"It's not the end," Troy said when he saw the sad look in Gabriella's eyes. He took her hand and spun her around. Then in a grand gesture, he dipped her like a ballroom dancer. "It's just the beginning!"

Gabriella looked at Troy and smiled. "This year has been really amazing, Troy. I wish it didn't have to end. But we have so many things to look forward to doing in the next few weeks. I'm just really glad that I get to share all of these special moments with you."

The rest of the Wildcats walked over to Troy

and Gabriella. "Three cheers for the Wildcats!" Chad yelled. The gang looked at one another and smiled. This would be a moment that they would cherish—forever.

SENIOR NOTES

Check out all of these
awesome senior notes
from your favorite
Wildcats.

East High Forever!

Dear Gabriella,

Thanks for making this the absolutely best year at East High. Working with you on the senior project has been so great. Once again, you pulled everyone together. Thanks for all your help with Rosie! We've still got some more memories to make . . . senior year isn't over yet. We've got so much to look forward to. . . .

Yours,

Dear Chad,

I should have known that you'd come through . . . you always do. Spending time with you this year has been a lot of fun. You're a crazy Wildcat, you know that? Thanks for my senior note. You're a slam dunk!

Best Always,

Dear Taylor,

You are probably surprised to get this note. Did you really think that I wouldn't write you one? Taylor, you are part of the reason why senior year has been so amazing! I've had a hard time expressing that to you. But you should know that I think that you're the greatest. Thanks for cheering at all our basketball games, and for making this year so special. This year would not have been the same without you by my side.

Always,

CHAD

Dear Troy,

Wildcat, you are
the best! You did
a great job at the
center with Rosie and
all the kids on the
team. I'm really
proud of you!
Thanks for making
this year full of
shining moments!
Yours always,

Gabriella

Dear Kelsi,

Great job on another musical! Your work on the show at the community center was the best. It was fun working with you and the kids at the center. You are the music master! I really hope that we can hang out a bit more before we graduate.

Your friend,

Ryan

Dear Martha,

The scenery for the Wellington Community Center show rocked! You not only can dance, you can paint, too! And the senior breakfast was a total jam. You rock!

From,

Jason

Dear Sharpay,
You are a star
director! You really
came through for
all the kids at the
center. Awesome
show! I think you're
really cool and are
so talented. Here's
to you!
Love,
Zeke

Dear Ryan,
Teaching the songwriting
class with you was so
much fun. You are really
talented-and funny! Love
those hats! Hopefully we
can spend some time
together before graduation.
Love,
Kelsi

Dear Gabriella,
The senior project was a huge success! Thanks as always for your great idea! You've added so much to our class, and you've been such a great friend. We've made so many awesome memories!
Love,

Taylor

Dear Troy,
Now you can add
basketball coach to your
resume, too! Nice job with
the center's team . . .
and with getting Rosie
center stage. As always,
you are a superstar.
Toodles,

Sharpay

Dear Jason,

Thanks for all your help with the senior breakfast. You are always a big help--and a great friend. Plus, you're a good dance partner, too!

Your friend,
Martha

Dear Taylor,
We did it! The
senior project was
fantastic. There
have been so many
great moments this
year, but working
with you at the
center these past
few weeks have been
so special. You
are a terrific
friend.
Love,

Gabriella

Dear Gabriella,
We did it! The show
was a great success!
Thanks for pushing
all of us to be part
of another musical!
You're a really nice
person and a good
friend.

Love,
Kelsi

Dear Zeke,

You are the sweetest!
Those pastries that you
left in my locker were
scrumptious! No one is
sweeter than you.
Hopefully we can
do lunch before
graduation

Hugs and Kisses,

Sharpay

Dear Martha,

It was so much fun working with you on so many senior committees this semester . . . not to mention the Scholastic Decathlon team! Your Wildcat spirit is red hot!

Your friend,

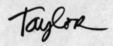

Dear Kelsi,

You did a wonderful job helping out with the kids at the community center—and especially with helping Rosie to come out of her shell and show off her stellar singing voice! It's been so much fun getting to know you and your musical talent is going to take you far.

Best Always,

Troy

Dear Sharpay,

What can I say—you did a really amazing job directing the musical at the community center. I know we've had our differences in the past, but I'm so glad that we were able to work together and put on a great musical for the kids. Here's to us!

All the best,

Taylor

Gabriella,

I must give credit
where credit is due—
your idea of having the
seniors volunteer at
the Community Center
was simply fabulous.
Who would've thought
that I'd be such a
great director? Theater
is truly my calling.
Toodles!

Sharpay

HIGH SCHOOL MUSICAL

CAN'T GET ENOUGH HIGH SCHOOL MUSICAL?

Collect all the books in the Stories from East High series,
original novels starring your favorite Wildcats!

DISNEY PRESS